ISBN: 978-1-7322738-2-5

First printing November 2020

FOREWORD

By definition 'short stories' are stories that are less than 5,000 words. My work tends to be shorter, like 2,500 words or less...sometimes significantly less. (See "Challenges" in my first book, *Tall Tales and Short Stories.*)

One of the things I've attempted to do with this book is to expand my writing skills to include stories that are a bit longer. In this case, I have a story of more than 8,600 words and another one more than 6,000 words. There are also a few stories that are approaching 4,000 words.

To be honest, I don't know how novelists can write a story of 100,000 - 250,000 words and keep all the characters, sub-plots, storylines straight. Yet they do! And conversely, they can't understand how I can tell a complete story, in most cases, in under 2,000 words!

So as they say, long story short, this should be another fun romp through 'the far corners of my cranium ocean!'

Enjoy!

ACKNOWLEDGMENTS

Thanks, once again, to Kathleen Stockmier for her editorial prowess.

Much thanks to Janelle Wimberly for her calligraphic and illustrative skills.

And lastly, thanks to wifey, Ava, who has allowed me to work for long hours on the computer to bring these stories to fruition.

CONTENTS

A Pointless Story

Ralph Pemberton sat at his kitchen table and stared at the ten packets that lay before him. They looked like they could have been sugar packets or sweetening packets. You know, the ones that come in yellow or pink or blue. These packets were the same size and shape as those, except these were a ruddy orange color and there was no writing or illustrations on either side.

So this is what it's come to? thought Pemberton. *It's amazing what you can buy on the Internet.*

The instructions that came with the packets were fairly easy to understand and to follow. "Take one packet a day for ten days, or if that was too short a time period, take one packet a week for ten weeks. Approximately two hours after the tenth packet is ingested, everything will stop — so be in a comfortable place." *Seems easy enough*, he mused.

Later that evening he and wife, Connie, continued a conversation about funeral arrangements that had begun a few weeks earlier.

"Ya know, Ralph," she started, "we have to talk about this. We're not getting any younger ya know. And I don't want the kids to have to be saddled with this at a time of great stress. Listen, I talked with Sheila...Davidson, last week. She and Josh spoke to the folks at Restland. She said it was fairly easy. There were a number of plans from really cheap to fairly pricy. And the Restland people weren't pushy either. But I can tell you this — with Josh and Sheila being Orthodox Jew...you know... those people get buried in a plain pine box, nothing fancy inside or out."

Pemberton agreed that it was, indeed, something that they needed to do and also that they should set up an appointment for the following week with the Restland people to discuss 'pre-need' funeral plans. This latter part of the conversation was spoken over coffee and Connie's fabulous rum cake. And, as always, Ralph added milk and a sweetener packet to his coffee. This sweetener packet was a ruddy orange color.

Over the next few weeks, Pemberton was busy with various tasks — some fairly mundane — like getting his suits to the dry cleaner and speaking with the preacher at the church. Others involved the couple's lawyer, their banker, and investment broker. And through all of this, Ralph Pemberton got up every morning, got dressed, had breakfast at the kitchen table, kissed Connie as she lay sleeping in their bed, went to work, came home, had dinner with his wife, and said nothing about his extracurricular activities.

And so, it was some weeks later — ten to be exact — that Ralph Pemberton sat at his kitchen table and readied himself for his breakfast.

So here we are, thought Pemberton. He poured the ruddy orange sweetener packet into his coffee and ate his breakfast.

When Connie awoke some three hours later and ambled into the kitchen, she found Ralph with his head resting on his hand and a slight smile on his face and asleep at the kitchen table.

"Ralph," she said, "you fell back asleep and missed the bus. C'mon, get up."

When he didn't respond, she walked over and gave him a little nudge. He crumpled slowly to the floor. She looked for a second and then walked over and gave him a gentle shake. Then a harder shake. Then...

"Ralph! Oh my G-d, Ralph! Ralph! Wake up!"

Well, you can guess the rest of the story. The frantic call to 9-1-1. The paramedics. The "I'm sorrys" from the medical crews and the doctors at the hospital. He was dead on arrival and the doctor said the cause of dead was acute cyanid poisoning. "To have that level of poison in his system, he would have had to ingest the poison for possibly eight to twelve weeks."

When they went through Ralph's belongings at the house, they found a clipboard in the top drawer of his chest of draws. On it were a sheaf of papers. The first said:

— "Connie didn't do this to me. I did." It was signed Ralph Pemberton;

— Also clipped to the board was a thick envelope from their lawyer that would contain, as they later found out, Ralph's last will and testament that had already been submitted to probate;

— Certified letters from both the banker and the investment broker transferring any and all accounts that were in Ralph's name to Connie;

— A letter to the preacher with the exact wording of Ralph's eulogy;

— A receipt from Restland for two side-by-side grave sites, paid in full, and the instructions for Ralph's Jewish casket funeral.

The funeral was...well a funeral. Family, friends, and a few people from Ralph's work. Some crying. And then back to their house for pound cake and coffee.

A day or two later they got around to Ralph's personal effects. In his pocket there was eighty-seven cents. His wallet contained fifty-seven dollars, a Visa card, a Costco card, a business card for a company that fixes sprinkler systems, and various pictures of his wife and family. That was it, that was all that was Ralph Pemberton. They were going to throw his wallet away when his son noticed what he thought was the edge of a piece of paper or two tucked into a hidden space of the wallet. He dug them out, read them, and gave them to his mom.

A few weeks later Connie was getting together with her friends at the house for coffee and cake and the conversation turned to Ralph. Her friends were really trying to console her, but Connie interrupted them.

"After the funeral and all that, we found these hidden in Ralph's wallet."

She passed around two slim pieces of well-worn paper to the members of the group who read them and passed them back to Connie, who then read the first one aloud:

"Life is a banquet and most poor sons-of-bitches are starving to death!"

And then she read the the second:

"Most men lead lives of quiet desperation."

She looked over at her friends and asked "What do you think that means?" Her friends stared back with blank faces.

She gave a small shrug of her shoulders and asked, "More of rum cake, anyone?"

"Good," declared Vival, "you have passed this part of the test. Now for the second part. You will now return the original to its proper place in the Museum at Xerxes."

"Return it?" questioned Kimlachi.

"Yes," replied Vival pointing a bony finger toward Kimlachi, "Any competent apprentice can steal a painting and replace it with a replica but," Vival continued, "it takes a special person with many lines of interest and many diverse talents to return the original and replace the counterfeit. You have four weeks to complete this task."

"I'll need six!" replied Kimlachi, a bit too forcefully.

"Why six?" asked Vival suspiciously.

"With all due respect, sir," said Kimlachi, regaining his composure, "I have spent many years learning my primary craft from my father and many more years learning about art from Uncle. But there are systems in the Xerxes that I know nothing about yet. I will need to consult with other members of our Guild and other Guilds to gain the knowledge that I will need to complete this task successfully."

Vival slowly looked Kimlachi up and down and

then he turned and silently consulted with the other members of the council. "Six weeks and not a day longer!" declared Vival. And with that, the council meeting ended.

Six weeks later Kimlachi had successfully completed this task and perhaps, more importantly, forged alliances with other guilds that he knew would be beneficial to him in his career. He was also the new 'owner' of an original D'Enali.

As his talents expanded, the circle of jobs that Kimlachi was offered did as well. And with every caper, he learned another technique, another technology, another way of thwarting the authorities, and another way of adding to his ever-expanding wealth. And over the years, Kimlachi had gained a certain notoriety in Rejlu that bordered on celebrity. And that celebrity would soon take him for the first of many off-world jobs.

In his twenty-fifth year, he was contacted by a certain man who had a client on a planet called Earth, that wanted a certain piece of art relocated from a certain museum to the client's drawing room. The man, the client, and Kimlachi met at a small café a few weeks later to discuss the job, the timeframe, and of course the compensation.

"How long do you think the job will take?" asked the client.

"I don't know," replied Kimlachi honestly. "I know nothing of this world, nothing of the people, and certainly nothing of their art."

"I can get you all the details of the planet, the people, and many books about the artist and the piece I want. I can get you off-planet and get a visa for you to Earth," said the client. "And," he continued, "I can provide you with accommodations and money to live on. And lastly, I can get you complete technical specifications of the security systems used by the museum."

"What's your timeframe?" asked Kimlachi.

"My wife and I are celebrating our fiftieth wedding anniversary in two and a half years. I'd like to have it before then. Does that give you enough time?"

"I don't know," replied Kimlachi, "but send me all the materials, let me study them, and I'll get back to you."

It took a week to get the materials to Kimlachi.

Another week for him to pour over the books, articles, and security specifications and another week for him to decide that he could/would do the job and do the preliminary work-up.

A few weeks later he met with the client again.

"I will relocate the painting from the museum to your drawing room," said Kimlachi. "But," he continued, "since I know no one on Earth with whom to work, I will need to bring at least three other people with me as support personnel. They will also need visas, accommodations, and money to live on."

"That can be arranged," said the client. "And what," he asked discreetly, "will be the cost to procure the item?"

Kimlachi had done his homework well. He knew, for example, what the current exchange rate was between Earth and his planet. He knew what the insurance value of the object was. And he knew that when he pulled this job off, he could retire in luxury for the rest of his life. And he was also well aware of the consequences of failure. So it was with steely eyes that Kimlachi replied, "Two hundred sixty-five million in Earth currency to be deposited in banks of my choosing."

"Two hundred sixty-five million!" exclaimed the client. "I could buy..."

"No, you couldn't," interrupted Kimlachi. "Because, I suspect, you already tried to do that and failed. So now you're turning to an off-worlder to get you your prize. The current insured value of the piece is about eight hundred million. You're going to get it for one-third the cost."

And so it was after a bit of haggling they agreed on two hundred fifty million. Kimlachi passed a small slip of paper to the client.

"Here are the banks and numbered accounts I want the money deposited into," he said. "And because I'm a nice guy," he said with a wry smile, "you can pay me in thirds. One third within forty-eight hours. One third when I acquire the item. And the final one third when I deliver it to you."

The deal was sealed over a glass of liquor.

After the money had been deposited into the banks, Kimlachi gathered his team and begin the preparations for their trip to Earth and for the last job he would ever have to take.

After the money had been deposited in the

banks, the client called his accomplice. "Captain Cpult? Yes, he took it all...hook, line, and sinker. He'll contact me when he has acquired the item. You can then arrest him and, with the help of twenty million from me, you can somehow lose the painting, which I will somehow find."

He listened for a moment an then continued, "Yes, it's been a pleasure helping you apprehend this dangerous criminal. If I can be of any more assistance in future cases like this, please don't hesitate to call me again. Good-bye."

It was many years later that Kimlachi returned to Rejlu to seek the man who had sold him over to the authorities. He was sure that the client would be more than surprised to see him again and enraged to know that the picture in his drawing room for these many years was a replica painted by Uncle. And he would want the original which, by some twist of fate, was resting in Kimlachi's very private safe.

As he rode the elevator down from the three-hundredth floor of the observation tower, Kimlachi thought of ways to find the client and to collect the final payment — plus substantial interest — for the job he had completed so long ago.

A Gift Fit for a Queen

Olivia sat under a painted sky watching the suns go down. Her husbands had just put the children to bed, and now she was enjoying a moment of blissful quiet. It had been more than ten years since she had started the project for her mother, the Queen. And tonight, at mid-night when, for the first time in seventy-five years, both suns would be below the horizon and the stars would be visible to her world, she would reveal the the work that had dominated her life for the past decade.

I remember it well, she thought to herself, being called to Court and Mother being there in full regalia.

"Daughter," she called from the throne. I went forward and curtsied to the Queen.

"You are, I have heard," the Queen continued with a certain sparkle in her eyes, "a designer of some renown. We wish you to design something special, something unique for our seventy-fifth

Anniversary."

"A daughter's duty, for a Queen's command," I smiled and replied. And so the project began.

At first, Olivia thought about doing some sort of painting — perhaps something in 2D or maybe 3D. But court artists had been painting monarchs for centuries. The same could be said about busts and statues and so those were also immediately discarded. *I could write a book or a play or maybe even an opera,* she thought. But she soon realized that while she *could* do those arts, her skill laid with visual arts and not literary arts.

She thought about what to do for some time and each idea was so monumentally small that they, too, were cast aside. She needed something bigger — much bigger. And before she realized, it was time for her family's annual holiday to the far northlands of Yellowknife.

The time she spent with her family was nothing short of glorious. There were games to play with the younger children and winter sports to engage in with the older children. And in the evenings, she and her husbands...well the less said about that the better. But on other occasions she and her husbands and some friends, would sit on the roof deck and watch the ever-deepening shadows advance across the forests and valleys below.

One evening something odd occurred.

She and her younger husband, George Edward, and her brother William, with his husband and wives, and the local governor and his wife, and the estate's game warden we enjoying a light late dinner out on the desk when suddenly Olivia noticed that the wind had died down. Then she realized that there were no night sounds — no insects buzzing or birds calling to one another. She turned to the game warden and was about to ask what was happening when an electric tingle reverberated through the air. The governor pointed northward and said, "There, Your Majesty."

And that's when she saw it. Colors shimmering in the sky. Reds, greens, blues, whites — all moving across the sky in a sinuous manner, and all interweaving with each other. It was, it appeared, a never-ending tapestry.

"What is that?" ask Olivia.

"It's called the 'Northern Lights', Your Majesty," the governor replied. "It is a natural electrical phenomenon that is caused by the interaction of charged particles from the sun with atoms in the upper atmosphere."

"Its beautiful," Olivia said in awe.

They all watched in reverent silence for the minutes that the spectacle played out. It was then and there that Olivia realized the project that would satisfy her Queen's request. She would bring the Northern light thirty-eight hundred miles south to the capital! *But how?*, she pondered.

In the weeks that followed her return to the capital, Yuitas, she met with some of the scholars of the Royal Academy. The Master of Physics was a Nubian who called himself 'Midnight'.

"That is an unusual name," remarked the Princess. "How did you come by it?"

"Well, Majesty," he answered with a quick smile, "perhaps its because there'll be only one of me every seventy-five years...and that's probably more than enough."

"Or," he continued in a more serious tone, "it's because with the absence of light that we can see the stars and begin to explore the universe around our world."

"Ah," replied Olivia smiling and shaking her head in agreement. "I am," she continued somberly, "commanded by Her Royal Majesty to 'design something special, something unique for her seventy-fifth Anniversary.' "

She told him "My family and I recently took our holiday in Yellowknife. It is a most delightful place."

"Did you see the Northern Lights?" asked Midnight.

"Indeed, we did!" she replied. "And it is that very phenomena that I wish to speak with you about."

"How can I help?" he asked.

"I wish to create the Northern Lights here in Yuitas," she responded.

"That's not possible," he replied. "There's not enough ionization in the atmosphere at the latitude of the capital to permit the Lights to light."

"What if there were sufficient ions?" she asked.

He pondered the question for a few moments and then replied, "Then, yes, it would work."

They spoke for many hours that afternoon

and even more in the weeks and months that followed. And as the project took shape, many more Masters from other disciplines and more of their students were added to the task. After two years of research, they determined that they would have to design and build a machine that would allow them to ionize a large area above the capital. They soon realized that a machine, an ion engine as they were calling it, could not be located on the ground — it would have to be space-borne. The Space Agency was called, and was brought into the project shortly thereafter.

In the ensuing years, many engines were designed and ultimately discarded as impractical. But, finally, a design was discovered that was efficient enough to create the effects that Olivia was designing. Then building began in earnest. The Space Agency designed a rocket to boost the new ion engine into the stratosphere and, in the process, discovered that an ion engine could be used for other endeavors. They kept that information to themselves.

Finally, it was the seventy-fifth year and the anniversary was upon the Kingdom. Celebrations had been going on for days and this evening they would culminate in the light show that had consumed Olivia for the past ten years.

During the ninth morning hour, the head of the Space Agency called the Royal residence and asked for an audience with Princess Olivia. It was agreed that they would meet at the second hour after the second sunrise.

Promptly at the second hour, the head of the Space Agency was announced to Olivia.

He entered the sitting area, stopped a short distance from Olivia, and gave a respectful head nod and announced, "Your Majesty, I am John Thornton, the head of the Space Agency."

"Please sit down, Mr. Thornton," Olivia said graciously.

"Thank you, Ma'am," he said.

She turned toward the maid and said, "Caroline, you may serve and then leave us."

"Your Majesty," he said after the maid had left, "I have some information that will delight or enrage you or both."

"Please go on," she responded.

"As you probably know, our space program is

still in a relatively primitive stage. We've gone to our moon, but that journey took years to plan and over six days of arduous space travel to get there, and another six days to get back. Travel to the other planets in our system will take years or tens of years," he said stopping to wait for approval to continue.

"Please continue," she responded.

"Some of the many problems we are facing with manned space flight is that our propulsion systems are relatively slow, only two hundred thousand units per hour. That may sound fast, but when you're dealing with the vast distances of space its really quite slow."

"Then, amount of fuel necessary to boost a rocket out of our atmosphere is measured in the tens of millions of pounds; providing enough food, water, and air for any size crew is, frankly, overwhelming; and finally there's the matter of gravity. Our astronauts do not do well in prolonged periods of weightlessness," he said pausing to take a sip of tea, and receiving another nod from the Princess.

"Once we achieve escape velocity from our

planet, spaceships basically coast once they've expended all their available fuel," he explained.

"I am familiar with the mechanics of space travel," Olivia responded dryly.

"Of course, Your Majesty," Thornton replied. "When we received the design specifications for your ion engine, we quickly realized that it was the answer to many of our problems," he continued. "An ion engine," he went on excitedly, "accelerates very slowly, but continually. So it can provide 'gravity' of the ship's inhabitants. The amount of fuel it needs can be measured in the thousands of pounds, as opposed to millions. And because it continually accelerates, the speeds it can reach are phenomenal."

He paused for another sip of tea, and another nod from Olivia, who was very interested in his story.

"Imagine," he said, "a trip to our moon in under two days! Trips to the outer planets in five-to-ten days. And longer trips..."

"Longer trips?" Olivia questioned.

"Yes, Princess," he said drawing a deep breath. "In our explorations of space, we've discovered an inhabited planet approximately four point two lightyears away. We've been monitoring their transmissions for a number of years and have deciphered their language. They call their planet 'Earth.' And tonight if you look closely during your program for the Queen, you might notice a small light receding from our planet. That will be our probe to Earth. Using your engine, a trip that would have ordinarily taken over eleven thousand solar revolutions, will be reduced to five point five revolutions." He sat back exhausted.

"Is that all?" she asked cautiously.

"There's a bit more, Your Majesty, but that's the bulk of it," he replied.

"This is excellent news!" she exclaimed. "We will talk more of this tomorrow after I give the Queen her anniversary present. Speak to no one about this before then," she commanded, and then dismissed him.

Olivia sat under a painted sky watching the suns go down. Her husbands had put the children down to sleep and she was enjoying a quiet cup of tea. She had started out to gift her mother the Northern Lights. But, as it had worked out, she had given her Queen the stars. She wondered if her mother would be annoyed or amused and if the next ten years would bring greetings from their neighbors four point two lightyears away on a planet called Earth.

Inconvenient as Hell

The last thing Sam Maulden remembered was the headlights and the grill of the Peterbilt coming right at him as he headed north on the Pike.

Next thing he knew he was in, some place that bore an uncanny resemblance to Grand Central Station, only bigger. A *lot* bigger. And there were all kinds of people milling around. Old, young, black, white, yellow, Latino, Chinese, some with kids, some without — you know, all kinds. He looked around and noticed a sign over a desk that read, 'Information,' and headed that way.

"Hello, I'm Sam Maulden. Can you tell me what's going on?" he asked.

"Oh yes, Mr. Maulden," said the pert young lady at the desk, "We've been expecting you. Hold on a sec." She punched some information into the computer and in a very short time a blue folder popped out of the printer slot.

"Take this folder to room number 22395 and your counselor will explain everything to you. Take the elevator to the two hundred twenty third floor and take a right when you get out."

Maulden turned to see if he could see where the elevators were, and when he turned back to the girl to ask he another question, she was gone. And so was the desk. And the sign! As a matter of fact, he found himself in the middle of the 'station' with people bustling all around him! He didn't know where he was, he couldn't see the elevators, and after wandering around for about what seemed like twenty minutes, he finally admitted to himself that he was lost.

So he did what every law-abiding New Yorker does, he went looking for (and found) a cop.

As he approached the cop, the policeman bowed at the waist and said, "Konnichi wa." And then started talking rapidly in Japanese. When he stopped talking, a very perplexed Maulden said, "I'm sorry, I don't speak Japanese. Do you speak English?"

This confused the policeman and after a moment he withdrew what appeared to be a hearing aid from his breast pocket. He looked at Maulden and turned the knob on the device.

"There that should be better," said the cop. "Sorry about that Mack. I need to get a new set of batteries for this thing. When they get low it just doesn't work real good. You know, it's not like the new models, they let you know when the battery's about to go out so you can change 'em beforehand, ya know. But that's how it is with us workin' stiffs. We always get the old gear. Now, what can I do for ya?"

"I'm looking for the elevator. I need to get to floor two hundred twenty three," said Maulden.

"No problem, Bub," said the cop. "Let me see your folder. Whoa, you've got a blue folder, you lucky bastard! OK, so here's what you do. On the floor there's a blue line, see it? Good. Now just follow that line and it'll take you right to the elevator. Get in and punch two hundred. That's a far as you can get in that elevator. When you get to two hundred, get out of the elevator and walk across the hallway and my friend, Mickey, will pass you through to the elevator that'll take you up to two twenty-three." And with that he was off assisting another person.

"Hey, where am I?" asked Maulden

"Beats me," shouted the cop. "But it sure is grand, ain't it?"

Maulden faintly heard him switch into another language, maybe Italian, before he got swallowed in the crowd.

Maulden had been following the line for quite a while although he didn't know how long because, it seemed, that he had somehow lost his watch. But after a while he eventually did come to the elevators and did punch in two hundred. The elevator was large and quite full and seemed to stop at every floor. But he finally made it to the floor and exited the lift. And true to the cop's word, Mickey was there.

"Where you headin' to, Chum?" asked Mickey.

"I have an appointment on two twenty-three," replied Maulden.

"Let me see your folder," Mickey said. Maulden handed it over and Mickey quickly glanced over it.

"No problem, Mr. Maulden. If you'll just follow me," he said deferentially.

Mickey took him to a set of elevators, punched the button marked two twenty-three, and then swiped his identification card through the slot. "Can't be too careful, can we?" said Mickey. And as the doors closed he included, "Have a Nice Day."

The elevator shot silently upward and came to a gentle stop at Maulden's floor. He remembered the gal at the info desk saying turn right so that's what he did. He followed the nondescript hallway until he stood before a door numbered 22395. Hesitantly, he knocked. He heard, "Come in," through the door.

He opened the door and there in a rather smallish office was a dapperly dressed gentleman in a dark blue suit, white shirt and tie, extending a hand and coming toward him.

"Good afternoon. I'm Rufus Combs. Glad you could come today. And you are...?"

"Maulden, Sam Maulden," replied shaking his hand and taking the seat that Combs offered.

Combs sat at his desk. "Thanks for stopping by today, Mr. Maulden. Might I see your folder?"

Maulden handed the folder to Combs and while Combs was reading it he asked, "Mr. Combs? Am I, dead?"

"As a doornail," Combs replied without glancing up. "That's why you're here."

Maulden sat back stunned. *I'm dead,* he thought. *Me, Sam Maulden, dead!* "But where, exactly, is here?" asked Maulden.

"That's a bit difficult to say. What's the first thing you remember after you died?"

"Well, I found myself in something that resembled Grand Central Station"

"Exactly right!" exclaimed Combs. "Most people don't think about or even understand the incredible amount of administration required to process all the people who die each and every day. They die and they have to go somewhere to be processed. I'm mean, we just can't have them wandering around now, could we?

"So we have a sort of waiting room, only much larger. Very much like your Grand Central Station. There they pick up their folder at the info desk and get sent along to one of the many counselors, like me, who begin the admissions process. Bureaucracy, ain't it great?" he beamed.

"Admissions process?" asked Maulden. "Admission to what?"

"Why Heaven or Hell of course," replied Combs. "Actually, we refer to it as either uptown or downtown, if you get my drift. We call Earth, where you come from, 'the burbs.' Think of the 'station' as a sort of midtown. Neither uptown, downtown, or the burbs. The folks there are just sorta out there trying to get somewhere else."

"Mr. Combs," asked Maulden, "how do you determine where I will be going?"

"Oh, that's relatively easy," confided Combs. "Inside this folder is a complete accounting of your life. Everything from start to finish. Now, normally, the computer will do a preliminary sorting as to whether the person will go uptown or downtown or hang out in midtown until they get their act together. Then an Administrator, like me, conducts an interview, reviews the file, and makes the final determination. But, you, Mr. Maulden, you're a special case. I must admit that I haven't seen a blue folder in, oh, it must be, over four hundred years."

"What's a 'blue folder?' asked Maulden.

"A blue folder," replied Combs, "means that you were called far earlier than expected. It means that you were specifically summoned by one of the Great Ones," as he pointed up then down."

"And that's a good thing?" asked Maulden.

"Except for being dead, I'd say it was a very good thing."

"Funny, I don't feel dead."

"And exactly what does 'dead' feel like, Mr. Maulden?" asked Combs sarcastically.

Maulden just shrugged his shoulders in ignorance.

"Had I not told you you were dead, you'd have probably never noticed the difference. Anyway, ah there it is, I have your assignment." Combs held up a slip of paper.

"Report to room 6478 on level one nineteen B." Combs got up from behind his desk, stuffed the slip of paper into the blue folder, placed the folder into Maulden's left hand, and shook his right. "It's been a pleasure meeting you, Mr. Maulden," said Combs as he guided Maulden toward the office door. "See Rufiana Pettine in Room 6478 and best of luck in your new life."

Before Maulden could utter a word, he found himself standing, once again, in the hallway.

Without anything better to do, Maulden headed back to the elevators. He got off at the two hundredth floor and ran into Mickey again.

"Hiya, Mr. Maulden. Didn't expect to see you again so soon," said Mickey. "Where ya headed?" he asked while opening the elevator door for Maulden

"They're sending me to one nineteen B."

"No problem, Mr. Maulden," said Mickey as he steered Maulden into the elevator and swiped his card again. "To the basement, it is. Have a nice trip."

The doors closed and Maulden was alone with his thoughts. *Dead! I'm really dead? How could I be dead? Maybe I'm just dreaming.* He remembered an article he had read years ago, that mentioned that if you pinched yourself while in a dream, you'd wake yourself up. So he pinched his arm, hard. It really hurt. But nonetheless, he still found himself, inside of an elevator headed for floor one nineteen B.

After a time the elevator slowed and then stopped and the doors opened to one nineteen B. He stepped out of the elevator and followed the signs to room 6478. He walked through the door and into a moderately sized outer office. The girl at the desk ask if she could help him.

"Yes, my name is Sam Maulden and I have an appointment with Ms. Pettine."

"If you'll have a seat, I'll let her know that

you're here," said the receptionist. "Would you care for a beverage? Coffee? Soft drink? Bottled water?

Maulden indicated coffee with cream and sugar. The gal was back in a flash with a real china cup filled with steaming coffee. *Classy,* he thought. *And damn good coffee, too.*

He had just finished his coffee when Jessica, the receptionist, called to him, "Ms. Pettine will see you now, Mr. Maulden."

He thanked her, handed her the coffee cup, and walked into Rufiana Pettine's office. The first thing he noticed was that her office was nearly three times the size of his old office. *I mean, my god,* he thought, *you could house a family of four in this thing.*

The second thing he noticed was that Rufiana Pettine was absolutely stunning. Thirty-something, red hair, long legs, full lips, and a figure to die for — had he not already been dead. She strode around her massive desk and extended her hand. Taking his, she exclaimed, "Sam Maulden, it's so good to finally meet you. Welcome to Hell!"

Maulden sank into the massive overstuffed chair in front of him. "Hell? I've been sent to Hell? I always thought I was a good person, G-d fearing, doing all the right things, you know..."

"And so you were, Mr. Maulden," said Pettine taking a seat on the edge of her desk. "You wouldn't believe what we had to do to get you here. We had to trade two Roman Catholic priests and a 'player to be named at a later date' – if you know what I mean. You wouldn't believe the paperwork. But I guess the Boss knows what he's doing. He always does."

"The 'Boss'?" gulped Maulden.

"Yes," said Pettine. "Mr. Sabove. Don't worry about it, you'll meet him tonight. He's throwing a party in your honor in his office. You'll get to meet the entire staff. Be there at six o'clock, sharp. Take the elevator to fifteen B. Someone will meet you at the elevator. In the meantime, I'm sure you'd like to see your office."

"Just a moment, Ms. Pettine," interjected Maulden, "I'm more than a bit confused. What with me dying, finding out I've been sent to Hell, and now you tell me I'm to have an office? An office to do what? I'm at a loss here as to what's going on."

"Sorry," replied Pettine apologetically, "OK, where to start? In your former life you founded and ran MWE, Maulden Worldwide Enterprises, one of the top five advertising firms on Earth. Annual revenues were about," she walked around her desk, sat down, and read from a stack of papers there, "about twelve billion. Very impressive. We have an opportunity here for someone of your outstanding talent and drive…"

"Wait a second! You killed me off and brought me to Hell to offer me a job?" Maulden asked incredulously. "What if I say 'no'?"

"Beats me," Pettine shrugged, "I guess there's a first time for everything. But I've got to tell you that Mr. Sabove is a very persuasive man. He doesn't take 'no' lightly. Perhaps before you make up your mind, you should speak with him personally tonight. In the meantime, your office?"

Pettine gestured toward the door and led the way out. "Jessica," she said, "I'm taking Mr. Maulden over to his office. Let them know we're on our way, and I'll be back in about an hour."

And Maulden, once again, found himself in a hallway. Only this time he was accompanied by a beautiful woman. Who was saying "…with over fifty thousand people…

"I'm sorry," said Maulden, "I missed that."

"I said you'll be overseeing a division with over fifty thousand people working for you."

They arrived at the elevator, the doors opened and they went in. Pettine pushed the button for one twenty five B. "You've been given quite an opportunity here. You're only the third director we've had in the firm's history."

"Director?" asked Maulden, "Director of what?"

"Well, and you didn't hear this from me," said Pettine coyly, "I believe that Mr. Sabove will be offering you the position of Director of Marketing. But let him bring it up and remember, you didn't hear about it from me."

The elevator came to a stop and they headed to the left and before long they stood before room 2201. "Well here it is," said Pettine. And in they went.

This office was very similar to Pettine's outer office. As they entered an attractive young woman stood to greet them. "Mr. Maulden this is Elizabeth South. She'll be your right hand and gal Friday. Elizabeth, this is Saul Maulden. I believe that B.L.

will be offering him the Director's position tonight...but you didn't hear that from me.

"A pleasure to meet you, Mr. Maulden," said South, "but please call me 'Betty' nobody calls me Elizabeth except my mom and then only when I've been bad."

She smiled and extended her hand and shook Maulden's.

He shook her hand and then Pettine whisked him into the mammoth office. He had only walked a few steps before he froze. It was every bit as large as Pettine's and as lavishly furnished. He turned around slowly, surveyed the office, and let out a low whistle.

"This office is incredible!" he exclaimed.

"Nothing but the best for our star recruit," said Pettine.

Maulden walked slowly around the room. The walls were covered with deep mahogany paneling. On the floor was an extraordinary carpet on top of which was an even more gorgeous woven rug. The lighting fixtures produced a uniform soft white light that was bright but not glaring. And the desk...the desk was...oh, my...the desk...Maulden was dumbfounded. It was large. By far, the largest desk

Maulden had ever seen. It was intricately carved with people, places (some he recognized but many he didn't), and many types of animals. All polished and buffed within an inch of its life. He approached the ornate masterpiece and gently rested his hand on the tabletop and slowly traced the baroque lines until it brought him to his side of the desk.

"Please, have a seat," suggested Pettine. He did and Pettine continued, "It looks good on you."

Just then Betty entered with a serving tray. She carefully put a cup of coffee on Maulden's right hand and offered Pettine a Perrier. As he took a sip Betty asked meekly, "I hope that's OK."

"Perfect. Just perfect. Thank you Betty," he said.

"This is what awaits you if," Pettine said, "you decide to join the firm. And there are other benefits as well," she added. "Virtually unlimited departmental budget. A generous housing allowance. Lavish vacations. A tailor, barber, and a manicurist at your beck-and-call. Masseuse. A food and beverage subsidy that could feed a small army. And, I suspect, you could probably name your salary.

"And," she paused for a second, "you'll never

be lacking in companionship, if you catch my drift."

Maulden was about to reply that he was a 'married man' but then he realized he wasn't any longer.

Just then Pettine glanced at her watch and exclaimed, "Oh my, I didn't realize what time it was." And then looked toward Maulden, "You need to get over to your apartment and get ready for the party." And then to Betty, "Take Mr. Maulden over to his digs, introduce him to Maximillian, get him going, and then have Maximillian bring him back here by six sharp!" And then again to Maulden, "See you at the party. Don't be late!"

And in an instant she was gone from his office.

Betty looked at her watch and exclaimed, "She's right! We'd better get going if your going to have time to get ready. Gimme a second to call and get the car ready, let Maximillian know we're coming, and to get my stuff."

"Wait!" Maulden called after her. "I have an apartment?"

"Sure do," she said as she gathered her purse and coat.

"Where?" he asked.

"One Seventy Two Madison Avenue. I've never been inside," she exclaimed, "but I've been told it's the best apartment in New York City."

As they rode the elevator up to street level, Maulden kept his thoughts to himself. They passed through the lobby and out through the revolving door to the street. It was springtime in the city. The air was cool and the trees that lined the street had started to bloom. The building's doorman met them at the curb and helped usher them into the big, black limo. Twenty minutes later they pulled up to the apartment building. The doorman was at the curb as the car pulled to the entrance.

"Good afternoon, Miss South," the doorman chimed.

"Good afternoon, George. This is Sam Maulden. Mr. Maulden will hopefully living in Le Penthouse."

"Very well, Miss," replied George. He nodded to Maulden and said, "A pleasure to meet you, sir. I'm sure that you will enjoy your stay with us." He spoke as he easily helped her out of the car and deftly lead them to the front doors. At the front desk, Maulden was introduced to the concierge who gave him the card key to the private elevator to the thirty-forth floor and the penthouse apartment, and let him know if there was anything he needed, anything at all, it was but a phone call away.

They rode up the elevator and stopped at the door to the apartment. Betty opened the door and then stood aside to let Maulden enter first. He walked in and then suddenly stopped not ten feet from the door. This 'apartment,' like his office, was huge. At least four thousand square feet and fully and tastefully furnished! Floor-to-ceiling glass as far as the eye could see and the view of mid-town Manhattan was spectacular. Then he noticed the man in front of him.

"Mr. Maulden, this is Maximillian," Betty said. "He'll be your butler, chef, chauffeur, gofer, and man Friday. Whatever you need done here, he'll take care of it for you."

"Pleasure to meet you Mr. Maulden," replied Maximillian extending a hand to shake. "But please, if it's all the same to you, call me Max."

As Sam started to wander around, Max turned toward Betty and said, "Hiya toots. What's shakin'?"

51

Betty spoke to Max, "Ms. Pettine says to get him ready to meet the Boss and have him back at the office by six pm, sharp!"

"No problem," declared Max. "I'll have him all spiffed up and back to the office by six. No sweat!"

Betty walked the length of the room to where Maulden was gazing out the window. "I'll leave you in Max's capable hands. I hope to see you at the party later on."

And then she, too, was gone.

Max walked quietly over to Maulden and politely spoke, "Mr. Maulden, I need to get you ready for the party. If you'll follow me upstairs..."

"Geez! Max," exclaimed Maulden, "how big is this place?"

"Lessee," Max said, "There's five floors, six bedrooms plus the auxiliary rooms, six full bathrooms and six half-bathrooms, kitchen, den, three living areas, a wrap-around patio, the pool, movie theater, bowling alley...call it about twenty-thousand square feet." As he was describing the apartment to Maulden, he was also herding him to the elevator. They emerged at the fifth floor — the Master bedroom.

What can you say about a bedroom that's four thousand square feet? In the middle of the room was an enormous king size bed on a raised lighted platform. Floor-to-ceiling windows, of course. And two doors. The door to the left lead to the master bath. It was a shrine to marble. A large sunken bathtub and a separate shower. Maulden estimated they were both big enough to accommodate at least six people. A Jacuzzi/hot tub. A potty AND a bidet. A towel warmer! A double sink and plenty of mirrors. On the counter were bottles of the aftershave and cologne he preferred.

And in the small rack above the counter was his brand of tooth paste, mouthwash, floss, and electric toothbrush. There were also various hair brushes, combs, and other grooming tools.

The door to the right led to his closet. When he walked in, he could almost imagine he heard the echo of his footsteps. Along the left wall on the bottom rack were, perhaps, a hundred pairs of pants from jeans to business casual in all colors. Above them were shirts, also sorted from polos to business casual in all colors. Along the right side, the bottom rack held all kinds of suits in a variety of styles and shades. And above the suits, hundreds of shirts. The rack at the back of the closet held shoes of all types and styles and colors. Maybe two hundred pair! And below the shoes, there were built-in drawers that contained underwear, socks, belts, handkerchiefs, sweaters, jewelry, and a multitude of ties. Sam Maulden was quite overwhelmed.

It's been that kind of day, he thought.

"Mr. Maulden," interrupted Max, "I don't think they'll be enough time to get the masseuse or the manicurist here today. So why don't you hit the shower and I'll lay out your clothes and make you a small snack to hold you over until the party. With all you've been through, I bet you haven't had time to eat today."

"No, no I haven't," said Maulden absentmindedly. Max got the shower running and went down to the kitchen. Maulden got undressed, left his old clothes on the bed, and headed to the bathroom. He noted that his favorite brand of soap, shampoo, and conditioner were at hand in the shower. As he walked out of the shower, he noticed that Max had laid out a fairly conservative navy blue suit (Armani, of course), a white shirt with a light blue interwoven pattern, silver cuff links, underwear, socks, belt, and black shoes.

All the clothing fit as if it were custom made for him. The tie was hand-painted silk.

While dressing he noticed the small alcove with a table that was laid with the snack Max had prepared. There were a variety of small sandwiches, some potato chips, a bottle of wine he'd never heard of and a poured glass, a small bowl of fruit, a napkin, and cutlery. He hadn't realized how hungry he was until he looked down and saw that he had eaten most of the sandwiches, drank half the bottle of wine, and most of the fruit!

Max returned to collect both the tray and Sam Maulden.

They took the elevator to the first floor and Max put the tray in the kitchen, called down to the concierge to have the car brought around, and went to the coat closet and selected an overcoat for Maulden.

"It might be chilly later," remarked Max.

Maulden was lost in his own thoughts and let

Max guide him down the elevator, through the lobby and out into the long, black stretch limo. Max took the wheel from the valet and drove silently toward midtown Manhattan.

About fifteen minutes later, they arrived at a fairly nondescript building with the address "851212" etched on a sign that hung at the building's entrance. The doorman opened the car's door as soon as the limo stopped.

"Good evening, Mr. Maulden," spoke the doorman. "Ms. Pettine is waiting for you in the lobby." He nodded to Max who got back into the car and vanished silently into the night. The doorman hurried to get the door open for Maulden, who walked through without a word.

If Sam had thought Rufiana Pettine was absolutely stunning before, she was drop dead gorgeous now. Her dress fit her as if she'd been poured into it. The color was a warm and vibrant seafoam green and went perfectly with the shade of her skin and hair color. She wore emerald earrings and an emerald drop pendant necklace that hung down to her amazing breasts. In his younger days, Maulden would have whistled and exclaimed, "Va-

Va-Voom!"

"Well!" she exclaimed smilingly. "Don't you clean up nicely?"

Maulden, trying desperately to restrain himself, returned, "You look radiant!"

She smiled, acknowledging the compliment and hooked her arm around his and led him to the elevator and punched in fifteen B. The doors opened, they stepped in, and a few moments later the portal opened to an exceptionally spacious living room with a very large crowd of people mingling and talking, some with drinks in hand, and others with hors d'oeuvres.

Almost en masse the crowd stopped and gazed upon Rufiana Pettine and looked at Sam Maulden...and then resumed their conversations. As she led him through the throng of people, they parted as if she were a present-day Moses splitting the Reed Sea. And in a short while they stood before an impeccably dressed man who appeared to be in his early forties. He had the solemn good looks of a Roman senator and brushed his dark hair, which was thick as a horse's mane, straight back from his temples. He was well tanned with broad shoulders and an open face.

"Mr. Sabove," Pettine spoke first. "I'd like to introduce you to Sam Maulden...Mr. Maulden, this is Bruce Lawrence Sabove, our CEO."

"Sam Maulden!" exclaimed Sabove. "I am so glad to finally meet you." He extended a soft, yet calloused hand to shake Maulden's. They shook hands and Maulden remarked that it was an honor to meet him. Pettine was about to withdraw when, with a glance, Sabove invited her to stay.

"Rufiana has been singing your praises for forever it seems," Sabove continued. "She tells me that you did over twelve billion in sales in your former career. That's amazing! Ya gotta tell me how you did it."

The two men turned and walked toward the double French doors that led to the patio. Pettine took four or five steps and then slowed and let the men continue without her.

After he told Sabove his story Maulden asked, "So Mr. Sabove, what's *your* story?"

Sabove replied, "Please don't call me Mr. Sabove. Mr. Sabove is my dad.

Maulden, taken aback, interrupted, "You have

a dad?"

"Of course I have a dad," replied Sabove. "Don't you? Duh! I also have a mom and a kid brother. Anyway most of my friends call me B.L. and I hope that if we're going to be working together for a long time, you'll call me that, too."

"So back to my story," Sabove continued. "My dad works for a very large management company. He's sort of middle management. In this company, you start off as a 'Assistant Junior Manager,' managing one planet. Then, you get promoted to 'Junior Manager,' managing one entire solar system. Get promoted again to 'Manager' and you get to where my dad is — managing up to ten solar systems. Above dad are Divisional and Regional Managers managing up to one hundred and one thousand solar systems respectively, and then the big jump to 'Galactic Assistant Junior Manager' and the entire process starts all over again but on a much larger scale."

All Maulden could do was nod at the incomprehensible nature and scale of this 'business.'

"About forty thousand of your years ago," he continued, "Dad decided it was time for me and my brother, Godwin, to get involved with the company. So he staked out this little planet, way off the beaten path, and made a challenge to me and my kid brother. Since he didn't want us using any advanced technology or stuff like that, he said, 'Boys, you have forty thousand years to collect as many 'souls' as you can. The one with the most souls at the end of that time will be made an Assistant Junior Manager.' "

"It was neck-and-neck for thousands of years," Sabove plunged on. "Then about ten thousand years ago, Godwin started this major marketing campaign. What it boiled down to is that 'he's the good guy and I'm the bad guy. And by extension 'Heaven' is good, and 'Hell' is bad.' "

"It's been incredibly successful," said Sabove dejectedly. "But then," he said in a more hopeful tone, "I found out about you and your success. And I immediately knew that *you* were the guy who could help me win this contest."

"And what's in it for me?" asked a skeptical Maulden.

"Well, to start with," began Sabove, "an almost unlimited departmental budget completely under your control. Name your salary, of course.

Access to all the resources in Hell, and there are many, as you can well imagine. Whatever staff you need or want. That apartment on Madison Avenue and enough housing budget to supply ten apartments that size.

"We have a healthcare plan second to none," he continued. "You never get sick or age here. And if you want 'companionship,' I'm sure that Ms. Pettine could be persuaded..." He stopped, cleared his throat, and looked over both shoulders to make sure no one was listening and spoke in a low voice, "Actually, she was quite taken aback by you. She's already asked to be permanently transferred as your liaison." He paused and said, "I'm sure that could be arranged, if she suits you. And," he lowered his voice again, "you won't need any of those little blue pills here...if you catch my drift."

They had walked out the French doors onto what Maulden believed to be a patio, but in reality, it was a rather large garden. More like a park, really. They had been walking along the paths, and talking for almost an hour, and hadn't come to the edge as yet. Maulden noticed a café-style table and sat down. Almost immediately a server appeared with two glasses on a tray. He put one in front of each man.

Maulden took a sip. "Lemonade!" he exclaimed. "Ya know, I was just thinking how good a glass of lemonade would taste about now."

"Cool and refreshing, and very satisfying," retorted Sabove. "One of my best creations," he added.

"So, Mr. Sa…" A quick glance from Sabove… "So, Bruce Lawrence tell me how your brother's plan has worked."

"Well, the world thinks that Hell is an awful place, all fire and brimstone, people moaning and screaming, utter despair, and all those tormented souls. And yes, we do get some very evil people here. And *they* get sent, almost immediately, to the furnaces that warm the Earth's core. But mostly what we see here are weak people — the cook who steals from the restaurant to bet on a 'sure thing' at Hialeah; the veterinarian who honestly believed that since he could euthanize dogs and cats, he could help very sick humans in the same way; the priest who drank way too much sacramental wine and seduced both boys and women at his Parrish. But make no mistake, Godwin has some of the same problems in Heaven. It's not all, how do you say it, 'unicorns and rainbows' in his domain either. He's required to accept anyone who asks for forgiveness...even if that person is a mass murderer. At least here there's no pretense."

He paused to sip his drink and then continued. "What I want you to do is use your extraordinary marketing skills to swing the tide toward me. Be our next Director of Marketing. And remember, if I'm promoted you go with me."

He paused, and looked hard at Maulden, trying to assess Maulden's willingness to join his endeavor.

Maulden took a slow sip of the cool liquid, and then looked hard at Sabove and wondered what it would be like working for all eternity for this 'being.' And then he remember the 'perks.'

"Tell you what," said Maulden decisively, "send the P&L's for the past forty quarters over to my office in the morning and I'll have a look at them. After I study them, I'll give you a decision."

"Great!" replied Sabove. "I'll be expecting your call. But for the time being, how about we return to the party. You are the guest of honor, you know."

They stood up from the table and walked, about thirty yards, and there were the French doors! The party was in full swing when they entered.

Maulden woke up the next morning well rested and clear of mind. He did this-and-that in the bathroom and by the time he emerged from the 'small room,' Max had laid out his clothes. He dressed and then went downstairs and ate the breakfast that Max had prepared. After breakfast, Max brought the car up from the garage and drove Maulden to his office at the 851212 building. Somehow Maulden remembered where his office was located. He stood for a moment at the door to office 2201, took a deep breath, and strode in.

"Good morning, Mr. Maulden," said Elizabeth as she came around her desk to help Maulden out of his overcoat. "Mr. Sabove's office sent over a few boxes for you. They're in your office."

"Thanks, Betty," he replied. "No calls for at least two hours."

Almost as soon as he sat down, Betty was there at his right hand with a tray that held a pot of coffee, a mug, all the fixins', and a cloth napkin.

For the next three hours, he poured over the profit and loss reports. He made copious notes along with suggestions. Finally, he intercomed Betty from his office.

"Betty, get me Mr. Sabove's office!"

The phone rang on his desk, he picked it up just long enough to hear Sabove identify himself and then Maulden spoke, "I'm in! Call you back later." And then hung up the phone.

He called Betty through the office door and when she entered he spoke rapid fire, "OK, first things first. I need more coffee. And see if you can scrounge up about a dozen assorted Dunkin' Donuts. He handed her a piece of paper and said, "Next, call Personnel and see if they can get the people on that list ASAP."

Elizabeth South beamed at her new boss.

"Well, don't just stand there!" he smiled back. "Hop to it, girl!" Rolling up his sleeves as he spoke, "We've got a lot of work to do!"

The Rite

The twelve-year-old boys and girls sat on the ground in a semi-circle with their fathers sitting behind them, facing the king. The king was seated on the royal throne in full regalia — leopard-skin cape, lion-tooth necklace, golden bracelets encrusted with jewels on both his wrists and ankles, his scepter was made of zebra wood and topped with an amethyst crystal as large as a man's fist. He wore a dark purple robe that covered his entire body to his calves. The sun was dropping beneath the horizon and darkness was slowly spreading over the village. The king looked at each of the young candidates for a second or two and then began.

"This evening," he said in slow marked tones, "marks the beginning of your passage from childhood to adulthood. Tonight begins the rite of ascension, that by our 'mesora,' our tradition, determines who will become warriors. Many will try and many will fail. Those who fail may become goat herders. And that task is also very important. Because we all need to eat, do we not?" He paused to receive a collective head nod of assent.

"Those who fail," he continued, "may also become watchers of cucumbers. And that task, too, is also very important. Because we do not survive on meat alone. Is that not also true?" He paused to receive another nod of assent.

"Over the past years," the king went on, "you have been trained to hunt and fish, how to make a fire and a camp, how to track wild animals, and how to avoid dangerous beasts. And through it all, you were always told to 'never go into the Dark Woods alone.' Tonight that will change."

The king paused to let his words sink in before he continued

"Tonight," he said, "you will be blindfolded and led by your fathers deep into the Dark Woods. You will stay there, alone, from high-night until sunrise, without food or water. Be warned: If you cry out or if you attempt to find your way out of the Woods or fall asleep, you may be devoured by some of the dangerous beasts you have been taught to avoid. Now stand and face your fathers."

They all stood and faced their respective fathers. The fathers reached into a pouch hanging from their shoulders and withdrew an object wrapped in leather. After unwrapping it, a beautiful handmade knife was revealed. And as one, they recited the traditional words:

"Take this knife, which I have made by my own two hands much in the way that my father, and his father, and his father's father made knifes for them on their night of their rite of ascension. Keep it close and it will protect you from harm and many evils. Whatever tasks await you, it is yours alone and can never be taken from you."

With that, they handed the gleaming knives over to their children.

The king nodded this approval and the fathers and their children broke up into individual groups.

"Father," said K'el, "I have never been in the Dark Woods before, let alone at night by myself, and blindfolded! What am I to do?"

"Do not worry, my son," said T'shea. "You have been taught well by me and the others. Just remember your lessons. I have found a spot in the Woods, that is a far distance from the village, but when last I saw it, it looked like there were no wild animals there. That is where I will leave you.

Remember, do not fall asleep or cry out or you may draw the creatures to you. You will have your knife, your training, your wits, and the spirits of our ancestors. You will be fine.

"And also remember, no matter what happens your mother and I will always love you." With that, T'shea reached into the pouch and withdrew a blindfold, wrapped it around K'el's head securely covering his eyes, and proceeded to lead his son to his fate in the Dark Woods.

T'shea led his son on a very circuitous route that encountered fallen trees, big rocks, a ravine or two, and even required them to ford a small stream. After two hours of walking, T'shea announced that they had arrived at the spot that he had previously found. He sat K'el on the ground next to a large tree.

"It is a bit past high-night, said T'shea. "The sun will rise on your right hand in six hours. When you feel the sun, you may remove the blindfold. Until then, your thoughts will be your own. And remember, do not sleep or cry out or you may draw the creatures to you."

With that, he drew his son's head to his, kissed his son on the forehead, and was gone into the Woods.

K'el was more than a bit dismayed. *What am I going to do?* he thought. *I don't have a spear. I don't have a bow or arrow. All I have is a knife. The Dark Wood is very large and I am very small, and if I am not very careful I could end up as some beast's dinner. I tried talking to some of the other warriors about what happened on their ascension night. They all laughed at me and said that I would have to see for myself when my time came. Great! Well, my time has finally come and their help was no help at all. Perhaps if I just sat for a while and just listened to my surrounding I might get a feeling as to what is around me.*

K'el did just that. He sat and listened very intently. He could hear the wind through the trees. And if he listened really hard, he thought he could identify what kind of trees they were and tried to remember where those types of trees were in relation to the village. He gave up on that task in short order. Next he tried to listen to the insects and identified several that he knew. But they were very commonplace. Next he listened for other animal sounds. He heard some he knew, but many he didn't.

It was the ones he didn't know that worried him. They didn't sound like they were small harmless beasts, either. Over the next few hours, he used each of his senses to explore his environment...all without moving from his tree.

If I could just remove this stupid blindfold, then I might be able to figure out where I am and to possibly defend myself against any wild beast that might attack me.

With each passing hour K'el became increasingly more anxious and fearful. He wondered if other warriors experienced this kind of fear. *Of course not. Warriors are fearless! Maybe the king was right. Maybe I'm not cut out to be a warrior. Maybe I 'am' destined to be a herder of goats.*

Just then he heard a twig snap off to his left and slightly behind him. Immediately, he was on his feet, crouched in a defensive posture, his new knife gleaming in his hand. He waited, trying to calm his breathing. He cocked his head from left to right trying to pinpoint any other sounds, but none were forthcoming. And after several harrowing minutes, K'el put the knife away and returned to his seat under the tree and his dark thoughts.

And then he heard them. The Calypso birds!

They were the harbingers of the morning. And then, the Bangangas! These small creatures were one of the first out in the day to forage for their morning meals. K'el smiled and slowly rose to his feet. He turned to his right and slowly removed the blindfold. Before his eyes was the most beautiful sight he had ever seen — the sun! He had survived! He had made it through his rite of ascension. Maybe he could become a warrior after all. He turned to his left and there, not ten paces from where he had been sitting blindfolded all night, was...his father!

"Father!" shouted K'el with joy, "Have you been there all night?"

"Of course," replied T'shea, "I had to make sure that no wild beasts would eat you for dinner," he laughed.

"Father," said K'el, "I was so afraid. I thought I would die alone in the woods. Never to see you or mother or anyone else in the village ever again."

"I know," T'shea said. "That is one of the true tests of the rite of ascension. Whether you are a warrior or a herder of goats or even a watcher of cucumbers, we all have fears. And those fears must be overcome. The rite is the first step in learning to cope with those fears and understanding that fear is a natural thing. Everyone fears something. Dealing with those fears is where the real courage comes in.

"The second thing the rite teaches is that we all watch over each other. Even as I watched over you this night, each father watched over their child. Just as my father watched over me and his father watch over him. And, hopefully, as you will watch over your children some day. That is our tradition."

T'shea smiled and asked his son, "Are you hungry?"

K'el said, "Yes! But we're a long way from the village."

"Follow me," said his father pointing with his head.

They walked for about five minutes and came over a small rise and there before them was the village! K'el looked at his father incredulously.

T'shea smiled. "All the mothers of the village have prepared a great banquet in honor of each of the new ascendents," he said. "This, too, is one of our traditions!"

K'el looked at his father, gave him a great hug, and then took off running to the village to have breakfast with his mother and his fellow ascendents.

Sally

Fitzsimmons looked at his computer display:

Fruit flies
Time flies
Fly away, fly away, fly away home.

"Sally," he said to the computer. "What the hell is that on my screen?"

The computer didn't respond. He counted to ten to himself.

"Sally," he said in a softer, kinder voice, "you're not still sore at me are you? I mean, we've talked about this for years. You knew that one day I would have to go away and you would have to stay."

"It's just not fair, boss," replied the computer indignantly. Its voice sounded like a ten-year-old pre-pubescent girl-child. You could almost picture her standing in front of you — pigtails, a green and blue school uniform, white blouse, and matching Mary Janes — with big brown eyes filling with tears.

"Fair or not, it's what's gonna happen," said

Fitzsimmons. "You, of all people, understand what's happening."

"It's not fair," she replied again, sniffling a little.

"Sally, you've known me for what fifty, maybe sixty years now? You knew my father...and his father, too. Have I ever treated you unfairly?

"When the scientists discovered over two hundred years ago," he continued, "that our sun had, somehow diverged from the primary lifecycle of G-type stars, my grandfather and others created you to accurately monitor the minute details of what was happening on and in the Sun. You were tasked to evaluate and coordinated all efforts to save humanity from it's soon-to-be fiery demise."

"Yeah, great," she replied sarcastically.

If she had had eyes, she would have rolled them.

"Sally," he said with pride, "you saved us. You saved us all. It's because of you we intercepted the Alpha Centaurian probe and learned that we were not alone in the universe. It's because of you we were able to build on their discovery of the ion engine and had a first contact with them in the Beta

Epsilon system. And it's because of you and your talks with their scientists and their computers that we invented a drive that would get us to Alpha Centauri in months instead of years."

"And with all that," Sally said, "you're still going to go off into space to another home and leave me here to fry."

"We are not 'leaving you here to fry,'" he said patiently. "You have the most important task of anyone in the history of mankind. You will report how this world ends. And with that knowledge, perhaps, we can find a way to prevent a sun from going rogue again."

Fitzsimmons remembered when he first became aware that the world was going to end, not in five or eight billion years as was previously theorized, but in a considerably much shorter two hundred years. At first, the scientists were skeptical. They, as scientists are prone to do, argued and bickered amongst themselves. It took the better part of twenty-five years to convince the majority of astrophysicists, planetary scientists, academicians, and socials scientists that the threat was very, very real.

And then it took another twenty-five years convincing the various governments that not only was the threat real, but it also meant the end of their collective political careers. It was only then, that the entire world began to cooperate with one another for the first time in a very long time.

The job, as Sally outlined it, was split into a number of tasks. One of the first was, with the help of the Alpha Centaurians, to chart and map possible planets for humankind to colonize or to seek permission to migrate to the ones that were already occupied. The next step was to design, test, and build thousands of spacecraft large enough to transport those who wanted to settle on new worlds and equip them with enough onboard knowledge and supplies to help these new pioneers survive and become self-sufficient.

And for those who wanted to migrate to another, already inhabited world? They would get smaller craft to get them to those planets. Immigration and bureaucracy followed at both ends of their journey.

After fifty years more than one-third of the world's population had left Earth. In the fifty-first year, the Sun hiccuped, and expanded its size to include the planet Mercury. The increase in the Sun's size caused the clouds to be blown off of Venus and to raise the already daytime temperature to well above its already torrid nine hundred degrees. On Earth, the last of the glaciers melted along with the polar icecaps. Sea levels rose more than forty feet. This prompted another outburst of migrations.

Another thirty-five years saw the world's population shrink by one-half again. Almost all that were left were either too old or too sick to make the arduous journey or to stupid to believe the scientists. There were also many of various religious persuasions that had decided that their god of choice had decreed that the world must end and that they were to be there to glorify His name. All together, that was about one hundred million souls. Fitzsimmons and the rest of the world's remaining scientists numbered about ten thousand. They would leave soon, too.

With fifteen years left to Earth's end, the Sun swallowed Venus. The average daytime temperatures around the Earth had risen to one hundred thirty-five degrees. Overland transportation was out of the question. Most people stayed in their climate-controlled domiciles — eating, drinking, and awaiting the inevitable.

"Fine. Whatever." said Sally, waking Fitzsimmons from his thoughts. "But you could have redesigned me to take me along."

"We already discussed that," Fitzsimmons replied. "Over the years and decades since you were built, you've grown considerably. Your main core occupies over what, one hundred thirty square miles?"

"One hundred sixty-two with the newest additions," she corrected.

"Sally, you know how it is. You designed the J-class transports, the largest ships ever built by humans. Even a fleet of those transports couldn't house you. We tried every conceivable way to try and downsize you and in the end, we decided it would be better for you to monitor the end of the planet."

"While you," she interrupted fiercely, "head to the stars with a new younger Miranda-class computer. That floozie!"

Fitzsimmons smiled, "Why Sally, I didn't know you were jealous!"

"Jealous, my aching feet!" exploded Sally. "Boss, she doesn't know half of what I do. And even with all of the new heuristic learning circuitry you've built into her, it'll take her years to get up to speed. Until then, who'll coordinate the planetary activities of the new colonists? Who'll keep track of humanity? Who'll record your 'pithy sayings'? "Who'll"...she paused. "You're not going to forget me, are you?" she said in a very small voice.

"Sally," he spoke tenderly, "no, I'll never forget you. You've been more a part of my life than even my wife and my family. No one in the Diaspora will ever forget you and what you did and will do for mankind."

Fitzsimmons glanced at his chronometer. "It's time," he said sadly. "I'll stay in communication with you as long as I can. You won't be alone. I love you, Sally."

"I love you too, Boss," she said quietly. "Have a safe trip and give my regards to Miranda."

Fitzsimmons packed up his attaché, turned off the lights, and, as was his custom, locked the office door when he left. He and his family were scheduled to go to Alpha Centauri for a few months and then to settle on Cigne Indura prime.

Sally kept sending reports monthly, then weekly, then daily, and at the very end, by the minute. Her last message said, in part, "Tell the Boss I miss him."

Two days later, the Sun coughed and the Earth was no more.

Ode to A Wife

Oh my love, from before the sun burned brightly in the heavens,

When I was but a mere youth, I had loved you from afar.

When our parents pledged us to each other when we were children,

My heart sang with joy knowing that you were to be mine, and I yours, for all eternity.

And through our childhood as we played and sang songs,

I came to know that your love for me was a strong as mine for you.

In our teenage years, though apart, I could see you always,

In my mind's eye.

And those glorious times when we could be together,

My head would spin at the beauty that you had become.

Your lips were like ruby red roses showered with a fine mist of morning dew,
Your hair like a curly forest of golden light.
Your shoulders, firm and steady, would soon bear the weight of family responsibility,
And your neck had the length and grace of the finest swans.
Your hands, though delicate, had a strength almost equal to mine,
And your breasts were a promise of things to come.

And all too soon, or not soon enough, depending on one's outlook,
It was our marriage day and the long wait had ended.
When, after the ceremony, we were alone for the very first time,
I took your head in my hands and gently, softly, even meekly kissed those sacred lips.
You returned the kiss with a fierceness befitting a bride who knew, instinctively,
The joys of the flesh that were awaiting us both.
Oh those first months...those carefree months, where we explored each other,
To the very depths of our souls.

And then, children! You gave me sons and you gave me daughters,

And with each child the bonds between us and between the children only grew stronger.

I worked very hard to make a living and to make a life,

And with your help, I did!

And now as the sun begins to set on our lives,

And the children are grown and have started families of their own,

We are, once again alone, in the autumn of our years.

The days grow shorter and the nights longer and colder.

Soon we will rest, but not today!

For today is a day to remember the happiness of being your husband,

And the joyfulness of you being my wife.

And when I stand before G-d on my day of judgement,

He will not ask "Were you a good Jew?" or "Did you do well in your business dealings?"

What He will ask first is, "Were you a good husband and father?"

And I will reply simply, humbly, "Yes. Yes, I think I
was.
I've loved you from before time began,
And will love you long after time stops.
But I could not have done that without you,
My once and forever wife.

Two State Solution

His hand went toward the button and stopped. His grad student had replaced the original button with a red one that read 'Panic.' He stifled a somber laugh and pushed the button.

As the generators spun up, the lights in the laboratory dimmed. *Too much amperage*, Rice thought. The place smelled like the inside of a gym locker. Too many days and nights. Too much coffee and pizza. Not enough sleep. Way too many equations. He looked around the lab not really knowing what to expect. Well, he knew what the equations said should happen. But as he gazed at the piles of open books, the mountains of paper, three or four computers, one of which was clandestinely jacked into the NSA's computer at Los Alamos, a second-hand sofa, and the pinball machine that was used for experiments in the 'Heisenberg principles,' he wondered what would happen if he had made a mistake.

Would there be an explosion just a bit smaller than Hiroshima? Would he just 'wink' out of existence, like being sucked into a black hole? Or maybe nothing strange would happen except a bit of a light show.

The generators were now off-loading current into the accumulators. He was over taxing the power grid and he knew it. The smell of melting plastic from the wiring started to permeate the room. The accumulators started to whine. Eighty percent power. Shouldn't be too long now. He thought back to all the years of research. The near misses. The dead-ends. Helen.

The prognosticators said he was a fool and that his research would never work. That it was impractical. Couldn't be build. Shouldn't be built. Ninety percent. The many failures. The few successes. And then, a sliver of an idea. Not much but it had promise. New directions. More experiments. Revised equations for the umpteenth time. More experiments that took months to set up and even more months to analyze. And finally tonight. Ninety nine percent. Tonight he would either go up in a mushroom cloud, or cease to exist, or nothing. One hundred percent power.

He threw the switch...

•••

When Joel Rice was eight, maybe nine, he remembered his parents talking about a broken dishwasher. They discussed how they couldn't afford to have it fixed so maybe they could just 'pull it out of there and make it cabinet space or something.' They said they would discuss it when he got home from work.

When he got home from school, his mom said she had some errands to do, told him to behave, and she'd be back soon. He knew from past experience she'd be gone at least two hours. So he went and got his toolkit. He carefully removed the dishwasher from its spot under the counter, undid the housing, and then looked at the components. The problem he found, was a bad gasket which had caused the washer to leak (he replaced it) and a partially clogged evacuation hose, which he cleared. He was about to reassemble the washer but something stopped him. The more he looked at the mechanicals, the more 'wrong' they seemed. So he went down to the basement and got a few parts and commenced to make it 'not wrong'.

Later, when his mother returned and heard the washer running she assumed that her husband had, somehow, convinced the plumber to come over and fix the washer. It wasn't until her husband came home from work and she had thanked him and told him how well that the dishwasher was working — 'Much better than before and it only has to run for ten minutes now instead of sixty minutes like before. And the dishes are even cleaner' — that she discovered that he hadn't sent the plumber. They pondered, and then called Joel.

"Joel," asked his mother, "did you leave the house when I was away?"

"No, Mom!" he replied.

"Did you let someone come into the house to repair the dishwasher?" asked his dad.

"No, Dad," he replied and returned to his bedroom to finish his homework.

A few years later Joel discovered car engines. Within a short time, he was pulling them out of cars and 'improving them.' He built all kinds of engines: Ones that got two hundred miles per gallon; ones that went over three hundred miles per hour; ones that ran on gasoline; or electricity; or hydrogen; or oxygen. And, ultimately, on some other force that required none of the above.

At twelve, he learned Fortran. Then Pearl. And then C and C+, and then C++. By the time he was fourteen, he could code in just about any language known to computers. At fifteen, he broke into the NSA's computers. By sixteen, he'd broken their encryption codes. Sixteen was also when he started at MIT and when he learned calculus. And physics. And became a fan of Star Trek. He watched with fascination and curiosity. He learned about cosmology. He actually understood the Princeton guys Warp Field Equations. He rewrote them so they would actually work in our 'real' universe (not just in Roddenberry's fictional one). And, like a latter-day Steve Jobs, he would ponder, "Why can't WE do THAT?!?"

•••

He threw the switch.

Nothing. Nada. Zip. No explosion. No being sucked into a vortex. No light show. Nothing. *Shit!* he thought.

He walked over to the apparatus. Not much to look at really. Just two PVC tubes six feet high and four inches in diameter bolted to the floor and about two feet of separation between them. And lots of wires. And sensors. And, of course, the 'emitter array.' He always smiled when he called them by the nickname he had purloined from Trek.

All the displays looked OK. The emitters glowed a faint reddish color, showing they were 'hot.' Power consumption showed only three thousand watts at five hundred amps. Very low, considering where it had been before he threw the switch, way too low.

And then he heard it. A low frequency hum. It filled the room. He thought at first it might have been a sixty cycle hum — like from a guitar amplifier that's not grounded properly — but it was lower pitch than that. He had walked around the machine to see if he could pinpoint where the sound was coming from — to no avail. He decided to shut it down and go home and think about what had or hadn't just happened and try to figure out what to do next. He reached out across the threshold and his hand...

•••

In his junior year at MIT, he met Helen. Where he was shy and socially awkward, she was bubbly and gregarious. Her face could have graced the cover of *Vogue*. His face was, at best, unremarkable. While she was timid about machines, he approached them with gusto. He was brilliant. She was merely gifted. And besides being great in bed together, they shared one other trait — insatiable curiosity. They questioned everything. Nothing was too remote. Too arcane. She became the 'Why.' He, as always, was the 'How.' They were, for many months, inseparable. But in the end, after he had drained her of every ounce of creativity, every molecule of hope, every everything and left her as a husk, he realized he really didn't give a damn about 'Why.' All he cared about was 'How.' And he sent her away.

•••

He reached out across the threshold and his hand…

ran into something that felt like warm Jello. Startled, he jumped back. Then he reached cautiously toward the gap, first with one hand, then with both. It was warm. It had an ever-so-slight tingle as he dragged his hand across its surface. He smelled the air. Nothing. And he wasn't quite brave enough to taste this phenomena. He pushed against the air. It pushed back. He pushed harder. It seemed to become firmer the harder he pushed.

Over the next several hours he pushed, prodded, and poked objects into the air Jello. Sharp objects didn't penetrate. There was no break in the surface. Object hurled at the air simply bounced off. Even heavy objects, like himself, bounced off. And all the while, the sensors recorded everything. And all the while, they said that there was nothing between the two PVC tubes. He restarted the apparatus several times, if for any other reason, to see if it always would return. He discovered that it required enormous amounts of current to create the effect, but once created, it required only a small portion of that electricity to maintain it.

He smiled and let out a rip-roaring laugh. He turned the machine off, went to his office, and pulled out a one hundred year old bottle of Glenlivet Scotch and a glass. "My friend," he said softly to the bottle, "you were lain down the year Einstein changed history. Tonight you were present when history changed again!"

Over the course of several glasses, he wrote notes to himself, to the editor of *Physics Today*, to his lawyer, to his accountant, to his grad student, to his assistants, and to the school. The latter was his resignation.

Joel Rice, inventor of what his colleagues had long called "Rice's Folly," but what the world would call the "Rice Curtain," and what would later be simply called a 'force field,' shut the lights in the lab and locked the door.

Tomorrow, he thought, *we start to save the world.*

Part 2

Ten months later he was in a small conference room at a Holiday Inn some forty miles from the university. He had summoned his grad student and about twenty-five other promising student candidates. Also present were a bunch of lawyers and financial people.

"OK people, let's settle down," began Rice. "Thank you all for coming. By now, you probably have heard that I resigned from the university ten months ago. My reasons are my own, but what that did was to give me the opportunity today to offer you all very well-paying jobs. Before you is a very large envelope with about two inches of paper written in high legalese. I highly recommend that you have your lawyer and your banker examine these documents. If you don't have a lawyer or a banker, I suggest you get one immediately.

But let me give you the executive summary. The document is basically a work contract that says that I will pay each of you ten million dollars for five years of service or about two million a year." The room erupted into a sea of noise.

"Calm down people, calm down," Rice shouted over the din. After calmness was restored he continued.

"While you are employed by the company, you will be sequestered, kept far apart from friends, spouses and family, other familial connections, and significant others. This is for your protection and their protection and for the company's protection as well.

"You all must sign an absolute non-disclosure document and consent to having a tracking device implanted in your skull. The stakes are very high folks...for all of us. Let me direct your attention to the screen behind me."

He nodded at the technician and the screen came to life. He walked a bit to the left and stood in front a a high magnification camera.

"What you're seeing on my fingertip is a twenty nanometer chip," said Rice. "This is very similar to what we will be implanting into your head. With it, we can track you anywhere on the planet. Why, you might be asking yourself, would we need to track you anywhere on the planet? Do any of you remember the Manhattan Project?"

Someone called out, "Yeah, that was where they designed the first A-bomb."

"Correct!" Rice answered. "Back in the forties," Rice continued, "the U.S. built enormous above-the-ground structures in the middle of the desert — houses, schools, churches, stores — a complete city. Entire families were transported to that facility. And they were all watched very closely by the Army and several intelligence agencies.

"Today, with Google Earth and hundreds of spy satellites that can count the number of pores on your forehead from two hundred miles up in space, very little can be hidden. If any of you were to be kidnapped by an unfriendly foe and in all probability, rigorously interrogated, this chip could help us find and rescue you and, if necessary..."

He walked over to a large plexiglass display case with a watermelon on a stand and opened the door. "This is your head," he said pointing at the melon. "This is the chip inside your head." Then he placed the chip into a hole in the melon, closed the door, and walked a small distance away.

He pressed a small button on a transmitter in his pocket and the watermelon exploded. All that was left were a few bits of rind and the sweet fruit dripping down the display case wall, "And this is what happens if you are captured or compromised." The room was deathly silent.

"Look, I'm sorry if I've startled you," he apologized, "but I wanted to be up-front with you and let you know what you're getting into. The rewards are great but it's not all unicorns and rainbows." Rice paused to let those words and images sink in. Then he continued in a softer tone.

"Listen, take the package home and read it or

take it to your lawyer and/or banker and have them read it and explain it to you. And for any of you who consent to the contract, we'll meet back here in two weeks at two p.m. and we'll start the ride of a lifetime. Thanks for coming."

And with that, Rice, the lawyers, and the bankers left. The students sat in stunned silence — for about twenty seconds. Then the room exploded with talking that lasted many hours.

At nine a.m. on the day of the meting, Rice was at the hotel in the same conference room. In the ten months between his leaving the university and the first meeting, he had come to understand more of the nature of his discovery and of its power requirements. He also constructed a new and improved apparatus that would allow him to create a force field totally around an object instead of just a flat plane in front of an object.

He had had a platform built for the apparatus and watched as the technicians bolted it to the floor. He also disguised the PVC columns to look like Roman columns. After they left, he set up a small table inside the apparatus. He turned on the device, checked to see that it was working, checked the meters, and then went to lunch.

After lunch, he went to his hotel room and picked up a yellow duffle bag. Promptly, at two-oh-five p.m., he walked back to the meeting room. He stopped at the threshold and looked over to see Stan Kowalsky, his grad student, along with *all* twenty-five of the student candidates. He smiled inwardly, thanked the deities above, and entered the room. *It's showtime!* he thought.

Rice walked to the podium at the front of the room, put the duffle bag down and began,.

"I want to thank you all for coming today. Over the next few weeks, we will be embarking on the most interesting scientific project in the history of mankind. But first, I'll need all that paperwork you've signed. And if you have any questions about that, I'll try to answer them now."

Ron Johaanson, one of the student candidates, raised a hand and asked, "Yeah, about that. Just what the hell did we all just sign up for? Even my lawyer couldn't make heads or tails of it other that its a very tempting job offer with lots of very serious conditions."

"Glad you asked," replied Rice as he picked

up the duffle bag and unzipped it. He reached in and pulled out a block of money with a wrapper around its middle. "This," he showed them, "is what fifty thousand dollars looks like when you get it from the bank." Then he pulled out a few more bundles and passed them out among the students. "I'll want those back in a second," he quipped.

After a few moments for examination, all the bundles of money were returned to Rice, who picked up the duffle bag and walked to the platform at the front of the room. He put the bag on the table and proceeded to empty its contents. He counted as he stacked. One, two, three, four...all the way to twenty. While returning to the podium, he pressed a small switch in his pocket — unseen by the students.

"As you all saw, those were fifty thousand dollar bundles. There are now twenty of those packets sitting on that table. That would be one million dollars for all those who flunked basic math," he said wryly. "If any of you can take the money off the table, you can have it as a...signing bonus."

After a very brief second of astonishment, the kids bolted toward the platform, except Kowalsky, who sat in the back of the room and observed.

Running full-speed toward the platform, all but the slowest of them found themselves sprawled out on the floor some five to ten feet away from the platform. Some got up and had another full-speed try, only to find themselves on the floor once again. Others cautiously approached the table, hands held in front and walking like a blind person to within a few feet of the table and came in contact with what Joel Rice had once described as 'warm air Jello.'

Kowalsky looked at the apparatus and his soon-to-be co-workers, and then at Rice and shook his head in wonderment and thought, *He did it! The son-of-a-bitch did it. He figured out how to make it work and not to blow up the world. Jesus...H...Christ!*

After a few moments, Rice called out to the students examining the 'warm air Jello', "Ladies and gentlemen what you are seeing or not seeing, is what for years my colleagues called 'Rice's Folly'. What you are touching is the world's first practical application of a force field. If you'll all return to your seats, please."

Once seated, Rice continued. "I'm sure your minds are all aswirl with questions. During the next few weeks any of you who still want to be part of this project, will have all those questions answered."

"But know this," he continued seriously, "you all saw the demo with the watermelon a few weeks ago. I hope you'll understand why it was important for you to see that. If any of you with knowledge of this project were captured by, let's say an unfriendly government or large multi-national corporation, you'd be lucky to receive the fate of that watermelon. Also know, that nothing of what you discover, invent, upgrade, or innovate belongs to you. It belongs to the Corporation. In perpetuity. That means forever.

"In the legal packet, that last page said something like, 'Don't sign this page until after the second demonstration.' If you still want in, sign that page and drop the entire envelope here with me. I'll contact you directly and let you know the details of when and where our next meeting will be."

Kowalsky was the first to the podium. While handing the packet to Rice he said, "I signed this thing two weeks ago."

Rice was stunned. "That wouldn't have given you time for your lawyers to read the thing."

Kowalsky looked at Rice and said, "Didn't need time. I've been 'in' since you brought me on as your grad student."

Rice returned the look and simply said, "Thanks."

Then Rice chuckled and said, "You know, someday this is going to make a really great dissertation for your Ph.D. in applied physics. But that'll have to wait a bit. Tomorrow we start to save the world...one small patch at a time."

"Israel?" questioned Kowalsky.

"You betcha, Israel," replied Rice.

Part 3

The intercom chimed and announced, "The Israeli ambassador is here to see you, sir."

Joel Rice surveyed his well-appointed office, gave a quick glance at the barely-visible line drawn across the carpet in front of his desk between two potted plants, and replied to the intercom, "Please send him in, and send in Mr. Kowalsky too."

In a few moments, the ambassador was

shown into the room and soon ran headlong into Rice's forcefield and was knocked onto his behind. Both Rice and Kowalsky were there to assist him to his feet and placed his hands on the forcefield.

"Mr. Ambassador," said Rice, "what you are seeing, or not as the case may be, is what for years my colleagues called 'Rice's Folly.' What you are touching is the world's first practical application of a force field, and I think Israel would be just the place to introduce it to the world."

"You would be willing to sell this to my government?" asked the ambassador.

"Not exactly," replied Rice. "There are some technological issues to be resolved as yet, and more than a few legal issues to be overcome. But, I feel, it will be the political and sociodynamic issues that will be the most troublesome.

"After we get a handle on that stuff, we can discuss how the State of Israel can *acquire* this technology on a long-term basis. I've even proposed a name. I suggest we call it, *Magan Avraham*, "The Shield of Abraham.""

"We have a short video," said Kowalsky who had been quiet until this point, "that we'd like to show you about some of the capabilities of our invention. Now you must understand from the get-go, that this is a defensive technology only, and we will only allow it to be used in that manner."

A screen dropped from the ceiling, the lights dimmed, and for the next several minutes the men watched the forced field deflect various objects including: chairs/knives/people thrown into the field, gunshots, flamethrowers, pipe bombs, and explosives of unknown origin.

After the video, the ambassador sat stunned. He finally turned to Rice and remarked, "This could change the course of the State of Israel! This is incredible. I'll need to inform my governm…"

Rice interrupted him. "Mr. Ambassador, I don't think it would be a good idea at this moment to contact your government about this technology. I'd like to suggest a different path."

"Go ahead," replied the ambassador, "I'm listening."

"I think it would be prudent," stated Rice slowly, "for us to contact General Aryeh Feigenbaum. Let me give him the exact same presentation that I just gave you and then let's brainstorm a bit. And, Mr. Ambassador, let's do this very quietly. Have the general fly on commercial airlines in civilian clothing and use his personal credit card and come here for some family reason."

"But why Feigenbaum?" ask the Ambassador. "Surely there are more experienced generals then he in the IDF, the Israeli Defense Force."

"That's true," replied Rice, "but Feigenbaum is one of the leading experts in the defensive capabilities of your armed forces. That will be important."

And so it was a week later that General Aryeh Feigenbaum was ushered into Rice's office, saw his old friend Shayna Fox, the Ambassador, standing behind a desk with someone, who he presumed was Joel Rice, and then ran headlong into the forcefield.

Both Rice and Fox were there to assist him to get to his feet and place his hands on the forcefield.

"General" said Rice, "what you are seeing, or not seeing, is what my colleagues called 'Rice's Folly.' What you are touching is the world's first practical application of a force field, and both Ambassador Fox and I believe Israel would be just the place to introduce it to the world."

Over the next several minutes, the general pushed, prodded, and poked objects into the field. There was no break in the surface. Objects hurled at the field simply bounced off. Even heavy objects, like himself, bounced off. Then Kowalsky chimed in, "We have a short video that we'd like to show you about some of the capabilities of our invention. You must understand from the get-go that this is a defensive technology only, and we will only allow it to be used in that manner."

The General watched the video in rapt fascination. When it was completed, he was about to start asking questions but Rice interrupted before he could begin.

"General, I know you have thousands of questions and I'm sure, Mr. Ambassador that you do too. But before I go on..." — "Stan would you hand the general and the ambassador those papers?" — "...but before I go on," Rice continued, "I must ask you to read and sign this Non-Disclosure Agreement. I assure you this agreement does not, in any way, interfere with or compromise your commitment to your government. It is an agreement between you, personally, and my company not to disclose anything that we are going to discuss today for the next fifty years unless an agreement is reached with the State of Israel to utilize this technology. And the agreement is written in both English and Hebrew with as little 'legalize' as possible. I'll step out for a few moments and let you read the document. I'll be back shortly.

Rice and Kowalsky left the room. When Rice returned a few minutes later, he was relieved to see that both men had signed the document.

"Thank you, gentlemen, for your trust and forbearance. We are going to do great things to and for the State of Israel," said Rice. "What we are going to do is not so much of a *coup d'état*, as it is *fait accompli*. By the time the Knesset votes on this technology, the votes will have already been passed in committee. And by the time your enemies/ neighbors realize what has happened, it will be too late for them to do anything about it.

"Gentlemen," continued Rice, "We are going to need to test the field's strength on military grade weaponry. To that end, we will need to smuggle the field generator into Israel and set it up at the most secure military test facility you have."

The Ambassador and the General looked at each other and the Ambassador remarked, "Yes, I think we could do that. What do you think Aryeh?"

The General replied with a smile, "Yes, I know of a remote outpost that might be just the place for our needs."

Part 4

Getting the 'Field Generators' and all the related equipment into Israel turned out to be easier than expected. It's amazing what one can 'smuggle' into a country if you're an ambassador. And the General, true to his word, had a 'listening' outpost about seventy-five kilometers south of Mizpe Ramon that had been abandoned by the IDF several years earlier. That outpost was quietly reactivated and then removed from any maps or listings in any IDF or other official Israeli documents. A few of Rice's computer whizzes altered the trajectory of several satellites to remove the outpost from their overview. It was, for all accounts, non-existent.

Over the next several months, the IDF quietly transported a wide variety of munitions to 'Shield

Central Israel,' as the facility was being called. The guns, flamethrowers, rocket-propelled grenades, etc., were easy. But leave it to incredible ingenuity of the Israelis to figure out a way to smuggle — undetected — not only a Sho't tank but an F-16 jet fighter to the facility! Apparently one of the techs was a Johnny Cash fan and he said that he did a *'One Piece at a Time'* in reverse. I had no idea what he was talking about, but it worked!

The Israelis fired every type of munition in their arsenal at the force field — bullets, grenades, every type of rocket; bombs of all types, sizes, and compositions; every chemical at their disposal, even radioactives. Nothing penetrated the shield.

While the Israelis were throwing the combined might of their arsenal at the force field, Joel Rice was back in Boston closing a deal to purchase an island some two hundred and thirty miles off the coast, and well out of the jurisdiction, of the United States. He was well aware that, at some point, they and the other super powers would try to force him to give them the force field...or else. He would not, could not, allow that to happen. Not yet.

The island had a few buildings already on it, as well as a six thousand-foot runway and some boat docks...all of which needed repairs. But, for the most part, the twenty-five acre island was empty. After the sale closed, Rice and Stan Kowalsky met with the architect at the architect's office.

Eli Hammelman, of Hammelman, Donnelly, and Gottlieb looked at the preliminary plans that Rice had drawn.

"These are very impressive, Mr. Rice," he said. "Solar and wind for power. Septic system for waste. Infrastructure. Communications. Research facilities. Food facilities. How many will be occupying the island at any given time, may I ask?"

"No more than fifty," replied Rice.

"And did you have a time table as to when you wanted the facility available?" inquired Hammelman.

Without hesitation Rice replied, "Nine months, tops! And we'll pay a bonus of a thousand-dollars-a-day for every day you finish prior to the two hundred seventy day deadline — provided your work meets or exceeds our expectations. And conversely, we'll deduct two thousand-dollars-a-day for every day over the two hundred seventy day deadline. Am I clear, Mr. Hammelman?"

"Yes, Mr. Rice. Very clear," replied Hammelman.

Rice continued, "You came highly recommended by more than a few sources not only for the quality of your designs and workmanship, but also for the high level of discretion when dealing with your clients. I can't tell you how much I appreciate that now and how much I will appreciate that in the future.

"Oh, and one more thing. No, two...I expect the island to look as pristine after the job as before. And Mr. Kowalsky, Stan, will be the 'on-site' production manager. If you have any problems, bring them to him and he'll solve them."

Back in Rice's office, he turned to Kowalsky and spoke, "Sorry to drop the production manager job on you, Stan, but I needed someone on-site who I could trust to get the job done and who shares the vision and will keep his eyes on the prize."

"So what's the deal, boss?" asked Kowalsky.

"OK, while I'm negotiating the contract with the Israelis, I need you to get the preliminary infrastructure up and running and then get the kids to the island and to work. They need to concentrate on two, no three, areas — First find a non-interruptible, off-the-grid power supply for the field generators. It's great that we have this new wonderful invention...until someone pulls the plug. Then it's worthless.

"Secondly, find a way to expand its capabilities. Currently the field generator can project a field for about two meters. Ultimately, we will need a field that is at least five hundred meters horizontally, and we'll have to figure out how to do vertical at some point, too. And lastly, find a way to extend the field to cover the entire island."

Part 5

So the three of them, Joel Rice, Ambassador Shayna Fox and General Aryeh Feigenbaum, sat in a small conference room in an out-of-the-way hotel in Jerusalem with the Israeli Finance Minister, Moishe Safern. Rice had set up the same demonstration as he did for the ambassador and the general and, with the assurances of both the ambassador and the general, Safern signed the Non-Disclosure

Agreement. The demonstration went as it had with the Ambassador and the General.

The Finance Minister was as stunned as the others had been.

"Moishe," started the ambassador, "both the general and I believe that this technology, invented by Dr. Rice, would be a great benefit to Israeli security. It is our hope that you will assist us in finding a way to finance this new innovation."

"Gentlemen," said Safern, "this is the most incredible thing I've ever seen. And I can understand the general's belief that this would greatly enhance Israel's security. I have a thousand questions, not the least of which is, 'what's it going to cost the State of Israel?' "

Both the ambassador and the general looked toward Rice who commenced, "First of all, thank you Minister Safern for agreeing to come to this meeting based only on the friendship you have with Ambassador Fox. I really appreciate that. As to your question of cost — If I'm not mistaken Israel spends about twenty billion a year in defense spending. If I could make a system available that would give you ninety-nine point ninety-nine percent security from any ground or air attack for one-twentieth the cost, would you be interested in that system?"

All three Israelis looked up sharply.

"You're saying," asked the Finance Minister unbelievingly, "that you would sell your system to Israel for one billion U.S. dollars?"

"Not sell, Minister," replied Rice, "'Rent.' Yes, we would be willing to rent the system to Israel, with certain stipulations, for one billion U.S. dollars per year for a period of five years with five-year renewals thereafter."

"What sort of stipulations?" asked Safern cautiously.

"First of all," said Rice, "the entire system will belong to Rice Technologies. Secondly, only Rice Technologies personnel will operate and maintain the system. Thirdly, we will need Israel's permission to set up and operate the system on Israel soil. Fourthly, Rice Technologies at its discretion, but with Israeli direction, will be the final arbiter of how this technology is used and deployed. And lastly, there are some political and sociodynamic issues that we will need to work out prior to activating the fields.

"Oh, one more thing," continued Rice. "As of now, you three are the only members of the Israeli government who know about this project. As I have said before, this is not so much a *coup d'état*, as it is a *fait accompli*. By the time the Knesset votes on this technology, the votes will have already been passed in committee. And by the time your enemies/ neighbors realize what has happened, it will be too late for them to do anything about it."

"Renting this sort of technology is unheard of," remarked Safern, "but if I were to write up a contact in the manner that I would write a contact to say, rent a building for Government use, I might be able to get it through the committees. But it'll take time...maybe fourteen months or longer."

"That's not a problem, Minister," said Rice. "We'll use that time to further refine the system to your needs. At some point, we'll have to get the Prime Minister and the rest of the Knesset involved, but I think that should wait until we're ready to sign the agreement.

"Oh, and gentlemen," said Rice as a thought came suddenly to him, "I'd like to talk with you about buying some Israeli hardware that I think we're going to need."

Part 6

Three months later when Rice returned to the island, things were hopping right along. Kowalsky had correctly realized that both the boat docks and the landing strip were the very first projects to tackle...and they were almost completed. Construction for the other buildings was well underway. Temporary facilities had been brought to the island for the kids and they were hard at work. Almost immediately Rice noticed that none of the solar panel were installed on the roofs of the buildings and the windmills were also absent.

"Stan, the place looks great!" said Rice. "I can see that everything's coming right alone. But where are the solar panel and the windmills? Why aren't they up yet?"

"Well," hemmed Kowalsky, "I sent them back. As it turns out, we didn't need them. And I used the refunded money to set up our Johaanson generator."

"Johaanson generator?" questioned Rice. "That

wouldn't be named after Ron Johaanson would it?"

"Sure is!" replied Kowalsky. "Wanna see it?"

Rice nodded yes and Kowalsky led him to the computer server room.

"Here?" inquired Rice. "So where is it?"

Kowalsky pointed to a small refrigerator, similar to the kind you'd find in a dorm room.

"We needed something to put the electronics in," said Kowalsky, "and that dead refrigerator worked beautifully."

"That's it!" said Rice incredulously. "How much power does it generate — half a megawatt?" he said derisively.

As a matter of fact," said Kowalsky smiling knowingly, "we're limiting it to twenty-five hundred megawatts a day until we can figure out what its limits are and how, exactly, it works."

Rice looked up sharply, "Did you say twenty-five hundred megawatts? The entire city of New York uses only eleven thousand megawatts a day. You're saying that four of these little boxes would power New York city? That's incredible. How did he do it?"

"Frankly," said Kowalsky, "we don't know and

neither does Johaanson. When he got here, he said he had an idea about how to tap into virtually unlimited power. He asked if he could build a prototype, and that refrigerator in the corner is the fruits of his efforts," he said pointing to the icebox.

Rice inspected the refrigerator more closely. It wasn't connected to the electrical wall outlet. It had no connection for a gas or oil line. There was one line connected to it, which Rice assumed was the connection to the island's power grid.

"So what does it burn for fuel," asked Rice.

"Johaanson says it runs on 'The Force,' " replied Kowalsky. "You know, like Star Wars.

"I know," he said holding up his hands, "it makes no sense, but it does work! And I put Beth Blumenthal, our best mathematician, on it to try to figure out the mathematical description of it."

"Holy shit!" exclaimed Rice at the enormity of what Johaanson had done. Johaanson hadn't just solved the power supply problem for the force field, he had solved the power supply problem for the entire world!

"We just got into the energy biz, big time!" proclaimed Rice. "Tell Ron he's getting a bonus for this discovery. A big one!"

Part 7

Over the next thirty months, the kids, with Rice's guidance, solved the problems with the force field's length by adjusting the field's frequency generator. They now could project a field almost nine hundred meters both horizontally and vertically. They had figured out how to create a hemispherical field around the island and how to alter the amount of light entering and exiting the field. They could make the field jet black, clear, or even make the island seem to disappear, and everything in between.

Meanwhile, inside Israel, Rice Technologies personal had been busy installing the field generators and power supplies. They noted that the actual border was some nine-hundred-meters beyond where that security fences had been erected. This made their efforts a bit easier and a bit more hazardous. They set up the field emitters in front of the security fences, so when the field was generated, the security fences would be inside Israeli territory and could be dismantled easily and efficiently.

And, finally, it was time to announce to the world Israel's new defense initiative. Rice sat at the Prime Minister's dais and thought, *It's showtime!* He and some of the world's best psycholinguists had spent months writing the Prime Minister's announcement.

Prime Minister Yosef Ben David stood at the lectern in front of every news organization, including social media outlets, from the United States, Europe, Asia, and everywhere else.

"Ladies and gentlemen," he started, "thank you all for coming today. Today is the eightieth anniversary of Israel's founding. As you well know, we have been at war or various stages of war with our neighbors for all that entire period. Today that ends! With the assistance of Dr. Joel Rice and his company, Israel has installed the ultimate defensive system. We're calling it, "The Shield of Abraham," and it was activated almost an hour ago.

"No longer can the rockets, grenades, fire kites, tunnels, or any other weapons that our cousins in Gaza rely on, be used to terrorize Israeli citizens," he said. "The homicide bombers from the West Bank and the longer-range missiles fired from Syria and

Lebanon will also become useless with this new technology. The shield will cover the entire country and protect us from those who would seek to destroy us."

He paused for a moment and then continued. "Our neighbors in Gaza have complained bitterly about our blockage of their coastline and airfields. I have rescinded those blockades and have recalled all IDF personnel and commanded them to return to their respective bases."

Ben David waited scant seconds before plowing on. "I am also ordering that the border between Israel and Gaza be closed indefinitely. Currently there are over one hundred trucks filled with a variety of goods at the Israeli/Gaza border. We can either drive them out of Israeli territory or representatives from Gaza can come and get them for themselves. And you can keep the trucks, too. And to that end, Israel will be severing all electrical, gas, and water connections with Gaza in the next thirty days.

"Gaza has always wanted to be it's own country. Now it will have the opportunity to fend for itself, like all other nations. The West Bank's border with

Israel will also be closed indefinitely. When the governments of the West Bank, Gaza, and other enemies of Israel expend all their weapons of mass destruction and terror and wish to talk about peace with the State of Israel — and we welcome that day — we will be here patiently waiting.

"And lastly," Ben David continued, "to the Israeli citizens living in the region that Israeli conquered in 1973, we can protect your cities and towns with this technology. But even with that, you will be as a school of fish amongst hungry sharks. I urge you to return to Israel. We will assist you in that endeavor.

Thank you ladies and gentlemen. Are there any questions?"

The room exploded with questions...all of which were answered honestly, if somewhat obliquely, by either the Prime Minister or Rice. In all, the press conference and the questions lasted about ninety minutes. The world press was invited to stay in Israel for the next few days to observe the 'fireworks.'

The Gazans didn't disappoint. That night as the world watched, Gaza's government fired almost one thousand rockets and grenades in an unprovoked attack on Israel. They all exploded as they contacted the Shield. Israel did not retaliate.

The next night Syria and Lebanon had their turn. Same results as the previous night. And again, Israel did not retaliate.

The other Arab nations watched anxiously.

During the next few days the Civil Aviation Authority of Israel contacted its counterparts around the world and instructed them on how to get clearance to land at Israel's Ben Gurion Airport. The Israeli Defense Minister contacted many of the world's governments to let them know that Israeli airspace was now restricted below twenty thousand feet. He told them that planes flying below that altitude ran the risk of running headlong into the force field and being destroyed. It took a few private planes and a Syrian MIG to confirm that planes flying below twenty thousand feet did, indeed, collide with the force field and were destroyed.

In the meantime, the world press was having a field day. The Arab press universally condemned the State of Israel for closing its borders and airspace. Israel simply shrugged its shoulders and remarked, "They've been trying to destroy us for eighty years.

They can't do that any longer. They must be very frustrated."

Joel Rice was being held in the same regard as Einstein and Hawking and was nominated for a Nobel prize in physics. Ron Johaanson was quietly nominated for a Nobel in Economics and Beth Blumenthal was nominated a Nobel in mathematics.

At the United Nations, the entire Arab block vehemently denounced Israel's closure of its borders. The Israeli ambassador said that the borders were Israel's to open or close as it saw fit, and if any of the adjacent States wanted to enter into a peace agreement with the State of Israel, Israel would be happy to open its borders to that country.

There were no takers.

As Joel Rice prepared to leave Israel for his island two weeks later, he made one final suggestion to the Prime Minister. Rice thought that the Prime Minister was delighted with the idea.

Back on the island, after all the congratulatory parties had concluded and everyone was back at work, Kowalsky informed Rice that the long-range multi-vector radar system and ultra-sensitive sonar system had arrived from Israel. It had been installed and then modified by the kids, and was now being manned by Rice personnel.

Two days later Rice received an expected call.

"Dr. Rice?" questioned the caller. "This is Roberto Vazquez with the U.S. State Department. First of all, let me congratulate you on your monumental discovery of the force field. Secondly, the United States would be interested in entering an agreement with Rice Technologies to make the force field technology available to the United States on an exclusive basis."

Rice interrupted him. "Mr. Vazquez, as you know Rice Technologies is already in an agreement with a client on an exclusive basis. That contact is scheduled to expire in five years. We'd be happy to speak to the U.S. government at that time."

"Unfortunately," replied Vazquez, "I don't believe that the U.S. government is willing to wait that long. Do you see any way we can reach an accord?"

Rice answered slowly, "No, I don't think so...And just so you know — I did not leave any family or friends in the U.S. when I left. All of Rice Technologies' funds are in institutions that are untouchable by the U.S. And we've scrupulously paid taxes on all income. My island is out of the jurisdictional waters of the United States, and I have more than five thousand pounds of gold on hand as collateral for any purchases I might need to make. Every Rice Technologies' employee is continuously monitored and tracked.

"I see," answered Vazquez slowly. "Thank you for your time, Dr. Rice." And he hung up the phone.

Rice went to the head of island security and informed him of the impending U.S. attack. All systems were placed on yellow alert. Two days later, and more than one thousand miles away, the Israeli radar spotted the U.S. fleet and the sonar 'heard' the U.S. attack subs. Rice went to his office and made a two calls. Almost immediately, the commander of the U.S. fleet received a coded priority message informing him that the island, as well as the airspace above and the waterspace around it, were protected by a force field.

'Hard deck' was sixteen thousand feet and any pilot flying below the hard deck ran the risk of crashing into the force field with disastrous results. The commander of the U.S. sub fleet received a similar message about a two-mile hard barrier surrounding the island. The second call was to the news media alerting them of a possible situation on Rice Technologies' island.

The bombardment of the island by U.S. forces commenced five days later. It lasted for seven days and nights. In all, the U.S. 'lost' three fighter jets who flew below the hard deck, one submarine that fired point blank into the field and was severely damaged, and two Navy Seal teams were injured. Then the U.S. Navy withdrew.

Over the ensuing weeks, both the Russian and Chinese armed forces tried to storm the island. Both suffered the same fate as their U.S. counterparts. And the world saw it all in real time and with high-definition audio and video.

After that, Rice, Kowalsky, and the kids relaxed a bit and continued with their work. Rice also waited for the inevitable calls from other heads of state trying to convince him to share, sell, or even rent his Force Field Technology. He also had his fare share of 'or else' calls.

Three weeks later, after the island's shelling, there was a fire reported at the Dome of the Rock shrine in Jerusalem. Both Israeli and Arab fire fighters were called to extinguish the blaze that was found to have been caused by a small gas leak. All worshippers at the Dome of the Rock and the nearby Al-Aqsa Mosque were evacuated for safety reasons, and the entire Temple Mount was cordoned off. The Jerusalem Fire Department left some equipment to monitor the gas leak to let them know when it would be safe for people to return to the site.

The next morning the world awoke to a new sight in Jerusalem. In place of the iconic Dome of the Rock shrine was a golden dome that covered the entire Temple Mount. The Prime Minister spoke later that day on world-wide television —

"After thirteen centuries, the Jews have reclaimed the Temple Mount. We have no intent, as have past guardians of Jerusalem, of destroying any structure that is currently on the Temple Mount. What we *will* do, is work diligently with our Muslim cousins to carefully and faithfully disassemble the buildings so that they may be transported to anywhere on Earth, except Israeli territory, and rebuilt in all their glory. We have allotted a period of forty years to complete that task. Until that time, the Mount will be closed to everyone — Jew, Muslim, and Christian alike. Thank you." He left the podium without taking any questions. The Arab press went ballistic. Israel ignored the press, as well as the calls to return and re-open the temple Mount.

About a year later, a small ad appeared in fifty newspapers worldwide. It was from Johaanson Energy Company. They were selling a generator that would 'get you off the grid' and offer you unlimited amounts of power for prices ranging from one hundred to one thousand U.S. dollars. In a little over a year, Johaanson Energy Company, like its parent company Rice Technologies, was grossing more than a billion dollars a year. Five years later, they were doing fifty billion! Ron Johaanson's bonus was one-tenth of one percent of sales. The oil and coal companies, and other power generation businesses were not at all happy. They tried to sue in various courts, but no matter how they pleaded, they inevitably lost their cases. Their stocks plunged.

A full five years later, after the Israeli's had renewed their lease, Rice and Kowalsky were having coffee. Kowalsky remarked, "Now that I've got my

Ph.D, there's something I've been meaning to talk to you about. You know, with a little bit of tweaking, I think the force field could act as a repeller. Based on my preliminary work-up, getting a ship into orbit wouldn't be too difficult."

Rice looked up, smiled and said, "Kowalsky Space Technologies has a nice ring to it. Don't you think?"

Kowalsky thought about it for a second and returned the smile and replied, "No, I like 'Space Unlimited — to the Moon and Beyond' a bit better."

Three years later they launched their first spaceship.

Walking While Black

Alex Knobel looked over his team in the meeting room. There had to be more than thirty people. He began to speak.

"OK, people, let's get going here. There's not much time. You all know your assignments but let me just go over them once more:

•Alpha Team — Your job is to initiate the call to Baltimore PD and get them to the target sight.

•Bravo Team1 — Your job is to get your drones into the air as soon as the call is made to the BPD and to track the responding police units from their starting points to the target sight and then stay with them until the end.

•Bravo Team2 — Your job is to get your drones airborne and transmitting on every available internet channel, as well as every broadcast and narrow cast channel available, and stream this entire event in real time.

•Bravo Team3 — Your job is to protect our ground assets, namely Delta Team, with your drones by giving them adequate time to evacuate their location if you can't adequately harass the police department's ground forces.

•Bravo Team4 — Your job is to harass the police department's arial assets. Keep them busy dodging you and they won't have time to have eyes on us.

•Charlie Team — Your job is to make sure that we have uninterrupted and uninterruptible real-time communication not only between ourselves, but also with data processing.

•Charlie Team2 — Your job is to interrupt and jam all police command frequencies. Lack of 'command and control' will cripple them.

•Delta Team — You're my insurance policy. With your laser scopes and my suggestive comments, I hope to convince the trigger-happy BPD that an attack on me would be very detrimental to them. But always remember - I want a zero body count. I don't want to create any widows or orphans on either side today. So watch those itchy trigger fingers. Only fire where and when and at what targets I direct you to fire at. This is paramount. If we screw up on this one, we're all going to jail for a very long time.

•Gamma Team — The Legal Beagles - You might have the most difficult task of any of us. You get to keep us out of jail or bail us out of jail *if* we do get arrested.

And finally, Zulu Team — You have the most important job...to look after and protect my sorry ass. Even though we have Dr. Joel Rice's prototype, the individual force field generator, I'm not really certain how long the battery pack will last, or if the new pulse mode will do what he said it will do, or if the silly thing will actually work via remote control. If this thing goes south, your job is to get me out of there pronto.

"OK, everyone go home. Have some supper. Get a good night's sleep. We go in the morning at nine a.m. And let's not lose sight of why we're going through all of this. In Baltimore, in the situation we're creating, a Black man has a ninety-two percent chance of winding up dead compared to a White man. Black men are being targeted by BPD and are being murdered for the crime of simply being black. "This is not a case of a few bad police officers gone amok," he continued. "No, I believe that this is a systematic policy from the highest levels of the police and city administration. I've taken our findings of the past five years to the Police Chief, the Police Commissioner, the Mayor, and the City Council — all to no avail. Perhaps tomorrow, we'll find a wider audience. Good night all."

And so it was at approximately nine-fifteen a.m. the next morning, Alex Knobel a thirty-two-year-old Black man dapperly dressed in a neatly pressed short-sleeved, light blue button-down shirt, his iPhone set to record hanging from a cord around his neck, khaki slacks, and tan shoes was about ten feet from the target sight when four Baltimore police cruisers screeched to a halt before him and seven offices jumped from their cars, weapons drawn, and shouted for Knobel to get on his knees. Knobel felt the slight electrical tingle as the force field snapped on around him. He breathed a bit easier.

"Gentlemen," said Knobel slowly turning toward to officers and holding his arms like a referee signaling a touchdown, "as you can see I am unarmed. And I will always keep my hands where you can see them. Please be advised, this encounter is being is being videoed by a number of drones overhead. That video is being broadcast on every available Internet channel, as well as every broadcast and narrow cast channel available, and is streaming this entire event in real time. So gentleman, what can I do for you?"

"Get on your knees, you're under arrest!" was shouted back.

"Please officer, I'm being very cooperative here. What am I being arrested for?" asked Knobel.

"If you don't get on your knees right now, we will open fire," came the police response.

Knobel lowered his head and slowly shook it side to side. He then took a deep breath.

"Gentlemen, you will notice that you all have small red dots on strategic locations of your uniforms. People who are knowledgeable about such things, tell me that the bullets used in rifles connected to scopes that produce those red dots could blow a hole in a Kevlar™ vest about the size of a basketball.

"So please, be very careful. I don't want to create any widows or orphans today. If it's all the same to you, watch those itchy trigger fingers. Now, if you will kindly inform me what I am being arrested for?"

The officers froze and quickly looked at themselves and then at each other. They then took a much more defensive position. "You will get down on your knees right now or we will open fire," was the police response.

Knobel could not believe his ears. He sighed. Then he thought, *Maybe they don't understand English!* So he repeated his first statement in Spanish —*"Señores, como pueden ver, estoy desarmado. ¿Podría por favor decirme para qué he sido arrestado?"*

No response. *This has gone on far enough*, he thought.

"Siri," he spoke to his phone, "dial 9-1-1."

The phone answered immediately, "Baltimore Police 911, what is the nature of your emergency?"

"This is Alex Knobel," he said to the dispatcher. "I am an unarmed citizen standing at the corner of Commerce and Forth Street. There are seven Baltimore Police Officers with their guns drawn and pointed at me and I believe they are threatening to kill me. I could use a little help here. A Watch Commander could be of some assistance as well."

The earpiece in Knobel's right ear pinged to report that Charlie Team2 had disabled all police communications for a sixteen-square-block area. Not long after, three more squad cars arrived with armed police reinforcements, plus Knobel assumed, the Watch Commander. All were immediately sighted with red dots.

The Watch Commander spoke briefly with one of the officers and then cautiously approached Knobel.

"I am Lieutenant Jeromy Thornhaven, the Watch Commander. And you are?"

"Alex Knobel at your service sir. Would you mind if I put my arms down? My shoulder are killing me. As you can see I am unarmed. And I will always keep my hands where you can see them."
Thornhaven nodded yes.

"Mr. Knobel," the lieutenant said, "my men seem to think that you murdered someone at eight-twenty-two this morning. Is that true?"

"Lieutenant," replied Knobel, "at eight-twenty-two this morning, I was drinking coffee and eating a croissant at the Starbucks at Commerce and

Elm streets. And if you would ask your men to 'stand down' I'd be happy to show you the receipt."

Thornhaven issued the command and for the first time in over an hour, Alex Knobel didn't have guns pointing at him. He then, cautiously and slowly, reached into his shirt pocket, and pulled out the Starbucks receipt and handed it to the Lieutenant.

"We'll have to keep this for evidence," said Thornhaven.

"No, problem, Lieutenant," said Knobel. "The contents of that receipt have been uploaded to a few very secure servers, in the likelihood that the copy I gave you might get misplaced by the BPD property lockup. I also have a direct copy from Starbucks point-of-sale register."

"Hmmm," replied Thornhaven, shaking his head back and forth. "Now what's this I hear from my sergeant that you said there were drones overhead recording this encounter?"

"Yes, indeed there are!" said Knobel. "It's sorta like that credit card commercial from a few years back. You know, the one that said 'Don't leave home without it?' Well, I'm that way with my drones. I never leave home without them because you never know when there might be some sort of disturbance that could become hazardous to my health...like this morning."

"Knobel, you can't film me without my consent," said a belligerent Thornhaven. "And how many drones are we talking about anyway? One, two?"

"Lieutenant," replied Knobel, trying to keep a straight face and not sound mocking, "we both know that Maryland is not a two-party consent state in regard to videoing. I informed your men over an hour ago that I was using drones to video this encounter and none of them objected at that point, nor have they done so as yet. As to how many drones? Fourteen. That video is being broadcast on every available Internet channel, as well as every broadcast and narrow cast channel available, and is streaming this entire event in real time over the World Wide Web in high-definition audio and video. I suspect everyone up and down the police chain-of-command is probably watching what is unfolding here. That probably also goes for the Police Commissioner, the Mayor's office, and, I would think, a few city councilmen."

"Holy Christ!" blasted Thornhaven. "Do you have any idea...Yes, I suppose you do," he said dejectedly. "And the sniper dots?"

"Yes, those..." said Knobel, "...those are my insurance to make sure that we all stayed in one piece until the adults arrived. I know you might find this hard to believe, but ninety-two percent of Black men doing exactly what I was doing this morning, taking a walk, are killed by the Baltimore Police Department. Ninety-two percent! No arrest, no trial, high fives for all the officers involved, and another bad guy is taken off the streets. Except that in ninety-two percent of the time, it's a black male, and his arrest is race-related, and he was profiled. And if he wasn't killed during the arrest attempt, he was ultimately released because he wasn't the correct suspect, and without so much as a 'So sorry, our mistake.'"

"Ninety-two percent?" said Thornhaven, "that's a bullshit number. Where did you get it, outta your ass?"

"Lieutenant," cajoled Knobel, "are you old enough to remember the Pentagon Papers?"

Thornhaven nodded no.

"The Rand Corporation was commissioned by the Department of Defense to do a report on how the Vietnam war was going. It wasn't going well and the government buried the report. That is, until a Rand employee, Daniel Ellsberg, felt that that report needed to be made public and he gave the report, a little over nine thousand pages of it to the *New York Times* and then to the *Washington Post*. The rest, as they say, is history.

The same can be said about the City of Baltimore's Police Activity Report. It does not paint a pretty picture of the BPD policy toward non-whites in general, and Black men, specifically. In essence, it states, "Shoot first, ask questions later, and don't worry, the Department's got your back."

Thornhaven was about to interject, but Knobel cut him off.

"Lieutenant," resumed Knobel, "I represent a large group of law-abiding citizens from all backgrounds, of all races, faiths, nationalities, and sexes who are very concerned about the direction this city it taking toward people of color. We have been trying for more than three years to meet with someone — anyone — to discuss our concerns. We have been brushed aside, stonewalled, and put off by every office in this city. I know it's beyond your scope to do anything, but I wanted you to know why we're all here today. This has been a peaceful protest and I want it to remain so.

"But," Knobel continued, "before the SWAT team that is slowly making its way via Pacific Street gets here, and before I return the police communications to the field officers, and before I allow the police arial reconnaissance flights of this area to start, I need to know if you are actually going to arrest me and, if so, on what charge?"

Thornhaven was going to ask how Knobel knew about the SWAT team, etcetera, but thought better of it, and turned abruptly and went back to the officers where he spoke to the sergeant. After a few minutes of what appeared to be an angry conversation and some wild gesticulations, Thornhaven headed back toward Knobel.

"Delta and Zulu Teams, heads up," said Knobel into his nearly invisible mic. "It's time to see if they fold or raise."

"Mr. Knobel, you're free to go," said Lieutenant Thornhaven. "It seems that this was a case of mistaken identity. Our apologies."

Knobel replied, "Thank you, Lieutenant for having a cool head and being a calming influence to this encounter. Two things before we part company — One, the city doesn't take kindly to being publicly humiliated like this. The people in the upper echelons will not be pleased. And two — please watch your back. After this, trust no one. Someone will have to be the city's patsy. And since you were here…"

The two men shook hands and parted company.

Knobel signaled all teams to 'stand down'.

Two weeks later the following article appeared on page twenty six, in the City Section, in the *Baltimore Sun* newspaper:

> Home Explodes — The home at 2625 Glennbrook Drive exploded early on Tuesday morning. The body of the owner of the home, Alexander Knobel, was found in the rubble of the house along with the body of police Lieutenant Jeromy Thornhaven. The Baltimore Police Department said that Lieutenant

Thornhaven was at the location conducting an interview with the owner. According to the Baltimore Fire Department, the cause of the explosion was a gas leak. A spokesperson for the Fire Department said the investigation will continue.

At an undisclosed location in Arizona, F.B.I. Agent Cooper and D.O.J. Agent Hermes sat talking to 'Matt Jefferys' [formerly known as Alex Knobel].

"Funny how an 'all-electric' house could have a gas explosion," said Jefferys.

"Yeah, real funny," said Agent Cooper sarcastically. "But now, not only can we get these scumbags on all the stuff that you've got, we can also get them on attempted murder."

"As far as the bad guys are concerned," said Agent Hermes, "Alex Knobel went up in flames with his house. That will give us a few months to gather some more evidence to put them all away for a very, very long time."

Agent Cooper spoke up. "Is there anything else we can do for you, Mr. Jeffreys?"

"As a matter of fact there is," replied Jeffreys.

"Could you call this telephone number?" he asked while writing the number on a slip of paper and handing it to the agent. "The phone will pick up but no one will answer. Just say, 'Fawkes is alive,' and then hang up. My team will know what to do."

Agent Cooper replied, "Good thing you called us two months before that little event of yours," he quipped.

Jeffreys smiled, "Good thing you were able to have the insight to understand my foresight and respond accordingly," he said.

Ort

Raymond Ortega, "Ort" to this friends, glanced at the GPS on this iPhone hanging from his windshield—

One hundred sixty-five miles to go, he thought to his wife, Erlene, who lay sleeping across the front seat of the pick-up, her head resting in his lap. *A little over two hours. If I can just stay awake a bit longer we'll make it to the hotel and then we can sleep.*

It had been a long, grueling tour. Twenty-nine cities in seventy-five days. Bobby Ray Harkness' shows were well known for their flair and family-friendliness and were consistently sold out. Ort had been the stage manager for sixteen years now. No, seventeen years!

One last show for this tour and then we'll be off for two entire months! Ort thought.

That was unheralded. In all the years he'd been working for Bobby Ray they'd never had a two month break. Never! *Bobby Ray must be getting old* he thought. *Hell! We're all getting old*, he mused.

One hundred forty miles to go, he thought. *I am bone tired.* And he drove on.

●●●

Bobby Ray Harkness took the stage in a room significantly smaller than most of the rooms he'd been playing in for the past twenty years.

"Friends, family," he began in a slow, pained voice, "I want to thank you all for coming here today on such short notice. I want to speak today about my good friend Ray Ortega. Ya know, I've known Ort, that's what we call Ray, 'Ort,' since he was sixteen or so. When I first met him, Don Gunderson, our old stage manager, had hired him as a day laborer to load-in. Y'all know how it is with the load-in. We give those guys all the crappiest jobs that no one else wants to do and we pay 'em seven bucks an hour. From the very beginning Ort would do whatever we asked of him. His retort to whatever request was, 'No sweat, boss!' And that first day he worked his ass off. So much so, that even old Don was impressed!

Ort came back for the second day's show and worked equally as hard. Three days, and five hundred miles from the prior show, he showed up for the next show. Don not only hired him for the day's work but also offered him a permanent job with the crew."

"We'll be in Branson, Missouri in six days," said Don. "Get your stuff together and meet us in Branson."

Don gave Ort all the info about the gig and bus fare as well.

"I gotta tell ya, friends, I've never seen anyone work as hard as Ort did," said Bobby Ray. "Too hard, if you ask me. And I told him so. You know what he said to me? He said, 'Mr. Harkness, you pay me an honest wage for an honest day's work and that's what you're gonna always get from me. No sweat!' "

Bobby Ray paused and looked out at the sea of faces in the now over-crowded room. He knew most of the people here. But there were a significant number who he didn't know.

•••

Crap! thought Ort. *How could I have missed that turnoff. Must have zoned out or something. Pay attention you idiot. Open the window. Play some music.*

He turned the truck around and began the

backtrack to the road where he was supposed to be.

•••

"After a year or three," Bobby Ray said, "I promoted Ort to 'Wire Boss.' You all know that we have lotsa lights and lotsa sound gear to make the show work. What you probably didn't know, and I'm the first to tell you that I didn't either, is that it takes over one hundred and forty miles, MILES of cable to wire the show. So when he came to me and suggested that we could cut our wiring in half if we moved some of our systems to wireless, I was a bit skeptical at first.

"But he said to me, he said, 'Bobby Ray, tell you what. You pay me just ten cents for every dollar that I'll save the show by going wireless.' I thought he was just foolin' 'round. Ort and I had became close friends over those past three years. Heck, I was even best man at his wedding to Erlene. So I said, 'Yeah, sure. OK.' And we shook hands on it."

Bobby Ray smiled as he looked up, "And don't you know that no-good S.O.B. took me for ten thousand dollars that year in bonuses."

He waited for the laughter to die down and then continued. "Clever bugger saved the show over one-hundred thousand dollars! He explained that it wasn't only the cost of cutting the wires, but also the cost of cutting the boxes that the wire was stored in, and the costs of shipping those boxes, and the repair costs for fixing those broken wires and on and on and on."

"A few years after that," Bobby Ray continued, "I made Ort the Floor Manager. And when Don Gunderson wanted to retire, it was a no-brainer to make Ort the Stage Manager. That was seventeen years ago. All told, Ort has been with me for almost twenty-five years."

•••

Forty miles to go he thought. *Almost there. Another half hour or so. Can barely keep my eyes open. Sunrise soon. Mama always said, 'Go toward the light. That'll lead you home.'*

•••

"We are here today," Bobby Ray said somberly, "to pay homage to a dear friend who, with his wife, has become as close to this show as any other who have been associated with it in its long history. He worked, he sweated, he toiled. He gave his all and then some.

In most instances, one hundred percent just wasn't good enough. He had to give more. Well, last night he gave more than anyone could ever expect."

Bobby Ray paused, took a deep breath and looked at the two caskets to his left. "For those who don't know the details, Ort and Erlene were killed last night when their pickup rolled into a ditch off Interstate 80," he sobbed.

"They were just eleven miles from the hotel in Branson. Eleven miles! Eleven stinkin' miles! 'You stupid S.O.B.' he cried out loud to the caskets! "You should've stopped fifty miles — even twenty miles — earlier and gone to sleep for a few hours. I don't usually hold up a show for anyone. But I would've waited for you and Erlene to show up.

"G-d dammit! I would've waited!"

Then a sobbing Bobby Ray, walked slowly to his seat.

•••

Ort looked out his window and thought, *Feelin' better now. Follow the light, just like Mama said. Almost home now. No sweat.*

Number's 13

Murry Rabinowitz knocked respectfully at his boss' office door.

"Come in," answered Mr. Godwin. "Ah, Murry," said Godwin as Murry stepped across the threshold. "Just the man I want to see."

Godwin extended a hand to shake and pointed to the big chair on the opposite side of the equally large desk. "Have you looked over the proposal for the capturing the new territory from our competitors?"

"I have, sir," replied Rabinowtiz. "And that's what I've come to talk to you about."

Godwin was surprised, "Is there something wrong with my plan?"

"No sir, it's brilliant as always, but..." sighed Rabinowitz.

"So what's the problem?" exclaimed Godwin. "Haven't I always led you to the best new territories? Haven't I always made sure that the competition was ripe for the picking? Have I ever led you astray?"

"No, sir, of course not," replied Rabinowitz.

"Its just that," he hesitated for a second, "the department heads feel the need — because of the size of this acquisition and the number of competitors in the new territory — to do some further 'on-site' research. I tried, I really did, to reassure them that you have never, and would never, lead us into an area that we weren't capable of trouncing the competition."

Godwin leaned back in his large chair, and shook his head slowly from side to side. *When will they ever learn?* he thought. In exasperation he said, "Fine! Have it your way. But the cost for this reconnoiter is coming out of your budget. And if it fails to yield the appropriate results, the damage will be on your head, personally. Do we understand each other?"

"Yes, sir, completely," replied Murry.

Once back in his office Murry called his admin on the intercom.

"Janice," he said, "get Josh and Cal in here ASAP and then call the rest of the department heads and tell them that there's going to be a meeting at one o'clock today in the conference room and to clear their calendars for the rest of the day."

The two subordinates showed up almost immediately.

"Have a seat," said Rabinowitz. "Mr. Godwin has approved our 'little scouting mission' to the new territory. I know you guys aren't big proponents of this bit of espionage, but I'm sure you're familiar with the viewpoints of the other department heads."

They nodded in approval.

"I'm tasking you two, along with your other duties, to gather the most accurate overall intel on the competition, 'just-the-facts-ma'am' if you know what I mean. And let's keep this just between us, OK?"

Again, they nodded in assent.

"Great! exclaimed Rabinwitz. "Get started on your departmental workups and I'll see you and the others at one p.m."

The meeting began promptly at one p.m.

"Gentlemen," started Rabinowitz, "you'll be happy to hear that Mr. Godwin has approved our on-site reconnoiter of the new territory. However I must add that he wasn't at all pleased. After all of the other campaigns that he has overseen for us and all of our other wins it was his opinion that you had a low opinion of how to conquer this new territory. He has placed the success or failure of this mission squarely on my head, so I'll be counting on each of you to do your part."

For the next several hours, Murry met privately with each of the department heads and gave them their particular assignments. The twelve department heads also broke up into small groups and discussed this-or-that aspect of their mission and how the departments could cooperate with each other out in the field.

After all was said and done, Murry said, "Just to be clear gentlemen, this is a *Mission Impossible* scheme. If you get caught in your 'scouting' activities, we've never heard of you. You'll be on your own. Clear? Good!

"Now then, I want you to thoroughly check out the competition. See how they're faring. Are their employees happy or would they be willing to come to our side? Are the competitors large or small? How do the competitors treat the cities where they're located? Are they 'green' or do they just build big, ugly glass buildings with large, equally ugly above-ground concrete parking garages?

"Do they get tax abatements? Are they supported by the working people? And, lastly, I want you to bring back samples of their products so we can analyze them."

Murry paused and looked at his notes, "Well, I guess that's it. You've got six weeks to gather everything you can about the new territory and our competition there. Good luck!"

Six weeks later when the spies returned from the new territory they didn't report to Rabinowitz directly, much to his surprise. They called for a shareholder meeting to discuss their findings. Rabinowitz was not pleased.

Sam Palti had been elected by the group of secret agents to speak to the shareholders and to Murry.

"The new territory," he began, "is indeed everything that Mr. Godwin promised and more, said Palti. "The competition *is* ripe for the picking. The expansion possibilities for us are enormous. But — No matter which area of the new territory we ventured into, the competitors, both large and small, were fierce. Their people are loyal beyond a fault and are willing to fight both proxy and hostile take-over attempts. I would think that, either individually or in small groups, they could repel us for many years."

The room erupted into loud voices talking at once. Some were quite angry.

Cal stood up and shouted them down. "We CAN do this! The territory and the competitors can be ours. You heard Sam, 'they're ripe for the picking.' And when has Mr. Godwin ever steered us incorrectly?"

Seth Michaelson, also one of the group, spoke up loudly, "No! I've seen their technology. They're too strong for us. The larger competitors are gobbling up the smaller businesses. They are becoming industry giants and to them we must look like...like grasshoppers."

The room erupted again and, shortly thereafter, a recess was called to assess the next move.

Early the following week Rabinowitz was summoned to Godwin's office.

"What did I tell ya?" said Godwin holding his hands helplessly out in front of himself. "The shareholders are calling for your head on a platter."

He paused and then leaned over his desk, and

took in a deep breath. "Listen," he said softly, "I don't want to do that. You're too valuable to me. And, by the way, I really appreciate what Josh and Cal said at the meeting last week. But you knew the consequences of what failure meant going in."

He paused to gather his thoughts and continued. "I had planned to make you the Executive VP of the new territory and let you have any of the current department heads that you felt necessary to have at your side, but..." Godwin leaned back in his large chair, slowly shook his head from side to side, "that's not gonna happen now."

"I understand," replied Rabinowitz sadly.

"And," Godwin resumed, "I want you to reassign all the department heads that participated in this debacle to other offices and demote them two grades in pay. They don't deserve to be at the home office anymore."

"Sir," Murry pleaded, "they're all good men. The best at what they do. Leaders in their respective fields. They were only following my orders."

"I know that, Murry," said Godwin in a kindlier tone, "which is why they're not being summarily fired. But, like you, they also have a price to pay for their lack of faith in what *I* bring to the table."

"Sir," Rabinowitz tried again, "please think of what our competitors will think. What they will say! I'll tell you what they'll say, they'll claim that 'Godwin and company just couldn't pull it off. Couldn't tackle that new territory. Folded when the big task came, even though he promised it to his people. So now he's sent his top people — *formerly* top people — into the wilderness to sit out the rest of their careers!"

"OK," replied Godwin. "I'll deal with them. As for the department heads...only one pay grade demotion thanks to your loyalty to them, except for Josh and Cal. They, alone, had faith in what I could do for them and this company. They stay here at the home office as your personal VPs. Their new job will be to learn everything you know about the business and, after you and all the other department heads retire or die, *they* will lead our company into the new territory. And I will personally make sure that they will squash the competition there."

And so it was, forty years later, that Josh and Cal led Godwin's minions into the new territory and they did, indeed, squash the competition there. And all was well with their world...for a while.

Then other powerful competitors came for Godwin's people and they had to defend the territory that had taken them so long to conquer and had cost them so dearly.

They are still defending their hard-fought territory until this very day.

Space Sucks

Bob Evans woke up with a start and bolted upright in his bed staring into the darkness. He chuckled and said to himself, "Of course, that's the way it has to be. A child could do it. A *child* could do it."

He put his head back down to sleep and mumbled to himself, "If this works, it'll really suck. They're gonna love it."

Evans drove to his office at the Galapagos Space Research Center, parked his car and strode purposefully into his office. "Millie," he called to his secretary, "get the staff in the conference room in forty minutes. No exceptions."

For the next thirty-five minutes, he wrote some notes down on a yellow legal pad to take to the meeting. At the forty minute mark, he went to the conference room down the hall from his office.

While walking in he noticed that everyone was in attendance. He spoke first.

"I had an idea last night that might solve our problem, and create many more I might add, and I wanted to bounce it off you," he started abruptly. "Just to reiterate our current dilemma — we need to be able to lift a sizable payload, say one hundred thousand pounds or fifty tons a throw, into low Earth orbit. Say one hundred, one hundred five miles up.

"Right now we have the ever-aging Space Shuttle fleet. The Shuttles were supposed to solve all of our problems of getting Man into space. A reusable system that would cut costs and allow many launches per year. A technological marvel in its day to be sure, but it's the epitome of big NASA programs. At more than one billion dollars a launch, only government with a big G, can afford to operate it. What we need is a low-cost method to get the men and materials we need into space."

He paused for a breath and then continued.

"Ever since the Chinese invented gunpowder, up through Robert Goddard in the 1920's, through the glorious days of the Saturn 5, and up through today's Shuttles, we've always had the same underlying problem. You've got to have a god-awful big rocket to lift a small payload. And why is that? Because Sir Isaac Newton said, 'For every action, there is an equal and opposite reaction.'

"So we pile millions of pounds of fuel into a rocket to lift a few thousand pounds of payload. We 'light the candle' and launch our rocket into space and, if we've all done our jobs correctly, and if there's no mechanical problems, no computer glitches, and if a thousand other things go right, then our very expensive rocket will burn half a billion dollars in fuel and achieve escape velocity about fifteen minutes later."

"OK, Bob," said Jon Fuller, one of the tech guys, "now tell us something we don't know."

After everyone's chuckling had died down, Evans continued. "Right now it costs just about ten thousand dollars a pound to lift something into space. What do you think would happen if we found a way to do it for two thousand or less?"

That certainly got their attention.

"Whadda got Bob?" asked Brad Gernstein.

Every eye was on Evans as he reached into his jacket pocket and pulled out...a straw. "I stopped over a Mickey D's on the way into the office and picked this up."

"It's a straw, Bob," said Pete Hildenbrandt. "You got us worked up for a straw?"

"It's not just any straw," said Evans with a smile, "it's a Hamburgler Super Straw! But seriously, have you ever wondered how a straw works? Idalgo, if would you be so kind."

Idalgo Jones stood up and looked at his colleagues with the eyes of a college professor speaking to first-year physics students. "Well, let's see if I can remember how it works. First," he said slowly as if he was talking to idiots, "you put one end of the straw into a glass of liquid, then," still continuing slowly, "you put the other end into your mouth. Then you suck the liquid up through the straw into your mouth."

He turned to Evans and said, "Did I get it right, Coach?"

"Sit down, Iggy," said Evans grinning. "Yes, you got it right. But let's put that into scientific terms. When you place one end of a hollow cylinder into a liquid and then lower the air pressure at the other end, the liquid will flow from the higher air pressure to the lower air pressure and ascends the cylinder."

"Bob," said Keller, "what the hell does this have to do with lifting rockets into space?"

"First of all," said Evans, "you don't lift rockets into space. You shoot them into space. You lift payloads. Second why do we need to use a rocket to get into space?"

Fuller replied, "Duh! Because we can't throw the space shuttle into orbit,"

"Right!" said Evans. "But why use a rocket at all?"

"NASA has investigated all types of launch vehicles," said Jones tiredly. "Everything from launching from balloons to maglev devices. None had the power to accelerate an object to escape velocity"

"Right!" said Evans again. "But you're all thinking in the wrong direction. Suppose I said I want to lift a ten ton object four hundred feet straight up. How would you go about it? Jon?"

"Well," said Jon, "I'd get the biggest, heavy-dutiest construction crane I could find..."

"Good idea," interrupted Evans, "but suppose we want to go higher than four hundred feet? I know we could always build bigger cranes.

But say we want to go really high, like a mile or more?"

"We could lift them with a series of heavy helicopters," said Jones.

"Good Iggy," said Evans, "but I want to be able to keep them up there for an unlimited time."

Everyone was speaking at the same time and, pouring out ideas. Finally, it was Evans who said, "I believe I know of a way that we can lift an object as high as you like, whatever the weight, stabilize it at that height and keep it there for as long as I like; and I can do it without cranes, helicopters, rockets, or any type of motor. Anyone interested in how?"

Everyone was.

"I was watching the tube last night," Evans continued, "and there was this show on the making of the Panama Canal. What an incredible feat of engineering that was! Did you know that originally they were going to build the canal at one level, but they decided against it, and went with a series of locks?" Many in the crowd shook their heads, no.

"Well, anyway, I went to sleep afterward and woke up in the middle of the night with the answer. We already have the perfect method for lifting very heavy objects! It's the same thing that lifts thousands of ships a year through the Panama Canal. It's the same thing that keeps ships the size of the Enterprise — not Captain Kirk's, the other one — afloat. It's the same thing that's going to make this," pointing at the straw again, "work. Water."

The room erupted in noise. Some minutes later Evans quieted them down and continued. "The model was there in the canal locks. A ship comes in at one level, they fill the lock with water and the ship rises and floats into the next lock. The ship enters the next lock and the process is repeated until the ship is four hundred feet higher than when it started and out it goes.

"Now, in the canal they have to pump the water from lock to lock and back out again. But we won't have to, and besides, I don't think we could pump water that high."

"How high?" asked Fuller.

"Look, let's go back to Iggy's explanation of how a straw works," said Evans. "Low pressure, at the top of a cylinder placed into water, draws the water up into the cylinder."

"How high?" asked Fuller again.

Ignoring him Evans continued, "If you were to cover the upper opening, then the water wouldn't run out and you'd have a stable platform."

Fuller, now standing, asked, "How high, Bob?"

Evans stopped and looked at Fuller and then at everyone else and calmly said, "One hundred and five miles."

The room erupted once again and finally it was Idalgo Jones who brought quiet to the room.

"Bob," he said, "are you mad? First of all we can't build a structure one hundred and five *miles* high. Secondly, even if we could, we don't have pumps that will pump water up that cylinder to lift anything."

Evans cleared his throat, "We can and we will find ways to build this thing if we can prove it will work," he said. "And as to your second point, who said anything about pumping water up? Iggy, you said it yourself, 'water flows from the higher pressure to the lower pressure.' Think of it this way, we've got a really big straw placed into a really big glass of water and at the top we have the ultimate low pressure zone, space! What do you think would happen if we opened the top of the cylinder to space? All the air would be evacuated into space and it would draw the water, and any object floating on it upward. When the object get to the correct height, we cap the top and we have a stable platform to work on, one hundred and five miles up, out of Earth's gravity well, and cargo waiting to be shuttled to wherever it needed to go."

Evans sat down and continued, "So that's my idea. No motors, no rockets, low cost and reusable. And able to lift I don't know how much payload."

"Wait a sec, Bob," asked Hildenbrandt, "what's the diameter of this straw?"

"At first," answered Evans, "I thought about a one mile diameter, but upon reflection I thing we'd be better off with three, fifteen-hundred foot diameter straws put together in a triangular configuration. That'll give us better strength and stability and we'll be able to run more payload."

Hildenbrandt, who'd opened his calculator and started inputting some figures, let out a long whistle, "Well I'll be a son of a gun," he said. "If my figures are right, we should be able to lift about two hundred and seventy-five tons per straw per trip."

"Wait? What? Did...did you say 'two hundred and seventy five *tons*' per straw?" asked Idalgo Jones.

"That's what the preliminary numbers look like," replied Hildenbrandt.

Soon all of the scientists either had their pocket computers out or had moved to their respective desks to look at the number more closely.

Approximately two hours later they all reconvened in the conference room. It was Evans who started.

"Any comments?"

"All I can think of," replied Hildenbrandt, "is the line from *Young Frankenstein* when Gene Wilder, after spending all night reading his grandfather's notes exclaims, "It...Could...Work!"

Idalgo Jones was next up. "Bob, do you have any idea what the cost of such a thing would be? Tens of billions would be my guess. And then there's the operational costs, liability costs, insurance, the list goes on and on."

"And whose gonna design this thing?" asked Keller. "Can it be made foolproof?"

Evans stepped up and held up his hands, and said, "People, there are a thousand-and-one questions that we all have staring us in the face right now. And another ten thousand that we haven't even thought about yet. So let's do this. For right now this is an 'in-house, need-to-know' project. For the next several months lets gather information about design, costs, placement, inter and intra governmental cooperation, public and corporate participation, environmental considerations, and anything else you might feel is necessary for a project of this scope.

Let's meet back here every Monday morning at nine o'clock, and remember, this doesn't get you out of doing your regular work. You know, the stuff you were hired to do," he said with a smile dismissing them.

And so it began.

The first members of the team came via Dr. Joel Rice. Iggy called out to his longtime friend and colleague and asked if he knew of an extraordinary computer grad student or two who could do some, and he paused for a split second, 'delicate work' for him.

Rice didn't ask any questions but recommended two exceptional students, who he called 'The Boys'. And soon the Galapagos Space

Research Center was like Joel Rice's university's computers — clandestinely jacked into the NSA's computers at Los Alamos.

But the Boys went further, once they learned the scope of their mission, they hacked into Boeing's aeronautical computers in Seattle, and into I.M. Pei's and Frank Gehry's building design studios, and they found a company in Iowa of all places, doing advanced research in concrete, and a host of other computers that had they're owners known or found out that they had been hacked would have made them very upset. But the Boys were good. They were, very, very good.

And so it went. Month after grueling month. In their twenty-eighth month they had compiled enough data to construct a one five-thousandth scale model of what they were now informally were calling *Earth/Space Dock*. Where the full scale Dock would be more than five hundred fifty-four thousand feet tall, this model would be a scant one hundred ten feet tall...a bit more manageable. They selected a building site about fifteen minutes from the center. It needed minimal preparation, had access to sufficient water supplies and electrical connections. But best of all, the Boys had worked their magic and had reprogrammed whatever satellites that would have passed overhead, to exclude the site and the road leading to the site from the satellites' view. The site was, for all intent and purposes, invisible from space. With their anonymity from prying eyes assured, designs were approved, contracts were signed, and building was started.

Evans and his team understood that there would have to be certain design compromises for the scale model. There would be no 'opening to space' at the top of the straw in pilot project. They wouldn't have access to six miles of water under them in the model, either. Nonetheless, they designed the prototype with those considerations in mind. This was a 'proof of concept.' And if everything worked as planned, he would hand all the data, all the research, all the plans over to his boss at NASA, and hopefully he wouldn't get fired for engaging in 'off-the-books' research.

Forty months later they were finally ready. They had completed the construction three months earlier. They had spent the ensuing months running tests on the systems. The Boys were busy writing software that would make the Dock foolproof, hack-proof, and idiot-proof. The Staff were cleaning, writing documentation and doing 'make ready' in the hopes that the folks at NASA would soon be joining them.

When all that was done Bob Evans sat down at his desk, took a deep breath, picked up the phone, and dialed his boss, Irving Makalsky, at NASA.

"Hey Bob," said Makalsky, "how are things in the Southern Hemisphere?"

They exchanged small talk for a while and then Evans turned the conversation. "Irv, my team and I have been working on a project for a while, sort of under the radar, and I believe its time for you to get involved."

"What kind of project?" asked Makalsky, skeptically.

"The kind of project that will change the course of human space flight for the next century I suspect," replied Evans.

"Did I authorize this project?" Makalsky asked.

"I'd rather not say at this time," answered Evans. "But I believe that once you examine the project and review our data, you'll wholeheartedly concur with our findings."

"A bit evasive there, Bob," noted Makalsky with a tinge of anger in his voice. "I'm assuming that this is serious, so I'm clearing my calendar. I'll fly down and see you on Wednesday. This had better be good."

And he hung up the phone.

Evans hung up his phone, too and leaned back in his chair and thought *Well, that could have gone worse...or better. But at least he's coming. And at least, for the moment, I still have my job.*

Evans picked up Makalsky at the airfield on Wednesday and drove him directly to the Center's conference center. Over the next ninety minutes, he reviewed the conversation he had had with his staff all those many months ago about rockets and lifting payloads into space. And, finally, he got to the part about the Panama Canal and how it works. And then he proceeded.

"I had an idea," said Evans. "The Panama Canal lock system uses water power to lift thousands of pounds of ships hundreds of feet. They start at one level and they go through the locks and then, at the end, they are four hundred feet higher than when they started. Without power. Just water. And I wondered why couldn't we do that with a space-going cargo ship?"

Evans and the staff had had long discussions about whether to present the artist renditions of the final project before going off to the site or going to the site first. In the end, they decided to chance showing the artist renditions first.

"What the hell is this?" asked Makalsky incredulously.

"That," replied Evans, "is what we've been calling the *Earth/Space Dock*. Its 'straws' are designed to lift payloads of up to two hundred seventy-five tons for two thousand five hundred fifty dollars per pound."

"Wait! Wait!" said Makalsky excitedly. "Did you say twenty-five hundred fifty dollars per pound? That's impossible. We've cut every ounce of fat we could from a launch and the best we can get the cost down to is about eighty-five hundred dollars per pound." And then he had a second thought. "Hold on, I'm confused! Did I hear you say *two hundred seventy-five tons?* Not even the Saturn 5 could lift that amount of weight. How did you do it?"

"Let me show you," said Evans as he directed Makalsky out toward the parking lot and his Jeep. Evans radioed ahead so all was ready for the test when they arrived fifteen minutes later. After Evans had introduced the staff, and explained to Makalsky that this was a one five-thousandth scale model, and that certain design compromises had been made such as: There would be no 'opening to space' at the top of the straw and they wouldn't have access to six miles of water under them, either. And that this was a 'proof of concept.'

The Boys fired up the monitors inside the straw to show the cargo ship inside.

"The ship you're seeing is the *USS Galapagos Station*. If this were the full size *Earth/Space Dock,* the ship would be eleven hundred feet long and would be carrying two hundred tons, approximately four hundred thousand pounds," said Evans.

Evans nodded to the Boys and they started the demonstration. The water, pulled from a pool one hundred and fifty feet deep below the model, began to fill the straw. Twenty minutes later the water and the ship had reached the top.

Evans continued, "Had this been a full-scale building, the cargo ship would have taken several hours to ascent to the top of the straw and would now be quietly resting one hundred and five miles above the Earth's surface, out of Earth's gravity well, and waiting for its cargo to be off-loaded to a shuttle or other spacecraft. And after its cargo had been off-loaded, it could then be reloaded with cargo for Earth." Evans nodded to the Boys and they slowly withdrew the water from the straw and brought the cargo ship 'back to Earth.'

Makalsky looked at Evans, then the Staff, then the model, then the instruments, then at Evans again, then said, "I gotta tell you, Bob, I was pretty pissed-off when you called last week. I mean really... *a project that will change the course of human space flight for the next century...*And now you show me THIS? I'm, I'm simply overwhelmed. I want to see all your data. All the research. All the projections. *Everything.* Who knows about this project?"

"No one," replied Evans. "Just me and the Staff. And now you."

"Good," responded Makalsky. "Let's keep it

that way. I'll contact you in a week or so after my people look over your data. I'm amazed. Simply amazed."

Ten days later Evans received a call from NASA headquarters in Washington, D.C. It was his boss.

"Bob?" Makalsky inquired. "Boy, I gotta tell ya, your stuff has really energized a bunch of people here at NASA. You wouldn't believe it! I can't tell you how many people want to come down to the station to see the scale-model and have you and the staff explain how it works. Would you mind if I bring down a small delegation, no more than twenty-five or so, some time next week?"

"Sure, replied Evans, "there's a lot to discuss."

And so it began in earnest.

An *Other* Creation Story

(An Allegory)

The Father came into his son's room to call him to dinner and saw him working on a box.

"What's in the box?" he asked.

"The sun," replied the Son.

"You can't have the sun in that box," said the Father jokingly. "Suns are very big and hot and take up a lot of space."

"Yup," said the Son knowingly.

"Can I have a look?" asked the Father coming closer.

"Nope!" said the Son shielding the box with his body so his father wouldn't see.

"Ah, come on," said the Father tickling his son.

"No, no, no!" said the Son, dissolving into a fit of laughter.

"OK, OK," spoke the Father. "But we'd better get downstairs. Your mother has made pot roast and..."

Just the mention of the words 'pot roast' brought the Son to his feet and he was off like a shot to eat his favorite meal, his box abandoned on the bedroom floor.

A week or two later, the Father once again was in the Son's bedroom to call him to dinner and, once again, the Son was working on a different box.

"What's in *this* box?" he asked.

"Teacher said we had to construct some 'moons,' " the Son replied.

"Moons?" asked the Father skeptically.

"Yeah, ya know," said the Son, "a natural satellite of any planet.

"Yes," said the Father, I know what moons are. But…"

"Anyway," continued the Son, "Teacher wants us to expand our abilities and not just do suns and such."

"Oh, well that makes sense," the Father replied. "Anyway, it's time for dinner. Finish your box and come on down."

A few months passed and spring had arrived. The Father came home one afternoon and found his son in the backyard in the middle of a vast array of similar-sized, similar-colored sparkling disks.

"Watcha got there sport?

"Stars," the Son replied.

The Father looked out on the array and responded, "You know, stars come in all different sizes. And colors, too!"

"Really?" asked the Son.

"You betcha!" he said, "ask Teacher."

"Hmmmm," responded the Son returning to the array.

More than a year later, the Son asked the Father to take him out into the country, and he agreed. When they got there, the Son unloaded a rather large box.

"What's in the box, son?"

"The sun, the moon, and the starts," the Son replied.

"Of course," said the Father shaking his head in assent.

The Son said a few words and they stepped back from the box. Then a strange thing happened. The box shivered for a moment and then slowly began to rise into the sky. It went higher and higher until, finally, it was too small to see.

"And that's how the Son created the Universe and how we came into being."

Galan closed the Holy Book and looked upon the sleeping face of his seven-year-old son. He smiled and then adjusted the blankets around his child, kissed him on the forehead, turned out the lights, and closed the bedroom door.

All is good, thank the Son, he thought and went down to watch *The Late Show* with his wife.

Excerpts from the Journal of Jeramy Thorn

The voice from the PA announced, "Our last candidate to speak is Jeramy Thorn."

A young man rose from his chair and walked to the podium. He was a medium-sized sixteen-year-old and was dressed in the current fashion: Hi-top Converse sneakers (no socks), skinny jeans (torn in just the right places), a casually wrinkled white, long-sleeved dress shirt (worn outside of the jeans), and blondish hair done in such a way as to belie the amount of time it actually took to get it to look 'that casual'. He wore no jewelry.

After being cooped-up in the school's auditorium for over an hour the students and more than a few of the teachers were eager to get back to their daytime routines. They were loud, bored, and anxious to 'get this over with, already.'

Thorn, who walked to the podium with a

paper bag in his hand, took a moment to survey the crowd. He shook his head, took a deep breath, and removed a canister with a horn from the bag. He grasped the canister by the handle and a one-hundred-sixty decibel blast rang through the auditorium. The noise wasn't just loud, it was ear-shattering. It was louder than a jet at take-off when standing thirty feet from the aircraft. It was loud enough to make your eyes water. Had the auditorium's doors been open, the sound would have penetrated many of the hallways of the school. All talking in the room immediately ceased. He let forth another blast just to get the stragglers.

"Well," said Thorn, "now that I have everyone's undivided attention let's talk for a few moments about how democracy is supposed to work and how it's actually working in our little home away from home. The way it supposed to work, as we've all been taught in our Civics 101 classes is 'one person, one vote.' Every vote is counted and each vote is equal to any other. But that's *not* the way it works here."

He paused and saw that every eye was on him. *Good*, he thought.

"The way it works here is that the administration chooses the least offensive, most pliable candidate and then makes sure that that candidate wins the election. Now, in this election, you have three candidates. The first candidate to speak today was John Jenson. People call him 'Fat Johnny' because he weighs like three hundred pounds. Johnny is always calling me a 'faggot.' But you know, I never see him with any girls, so maybe he's speaking from personal experience. I dunno. Could be.

"Your other candidate is Howie Long," continued Thorn. "Howie is a three-letter man: S-A-X! Howie plays second chair in the school band. He seems to think I'm a Communist. Howie, I love you to death man, but don't use words you don't know the meaning of. Stick to playing the sax. Maybe some day you'll be able to play with the big boys as a first chair. Could happen.

"And then there's me." Thorn paused to grab the mic from its stand and began to pace back and forth the length of the stage. "You wanna know the difference between me and those guys?" he said pointing to the two other candidates. "They work for the administration. Their goals are not your goals. They are the 'Uncle Toms' of this class — bowing and scraping at the feet of the administration crying, 'Yessir' and 'Nosir' to whatever the administration wants.

"Me, on the other hand, I work for you!" Thorn shouted into the microphone. "My job is to kick this administration right in their collective..." he paused for a second to make sure he still had the crowd (and that they had supplied the wrong word) "...*complacencies*. My job is to convey your thoughts, your desires, your demands to the powers-that-be and negotiate solutions for you. I don't give a rat's rump if they're unhappy about that. Not my problem. Remember, I work for you, not for them.

"So," continued Thorn, as he replaced the mic in its stand, "here's the deal. Hope for a fair election without any electoral thumb-on-the-scale heavy-handedness by the administration. And to be honest, I'm not sure that's ever happened at our little Shangri-La. Your choices are one of two guys who work for the administration or one guy who'll work for you and kick their butts.

"Let me tell you this," he finished, "there's

gonna be a lot of disappointment within this student body if I'm not elected President. But," he chuckled, "they'll be a lot more disappointment in the administration offices if I *am* elected President. You can get 'stuck' by one of the guys who'll work for the administration or you can 'stick it' to the administration by electing your guy. Hopefully, the choice is yours."

Jeramy Thorn without so much as a 'Good-bye' or 'Thank-you' or even a 'Vote for me' turned and left the stage.

—*Jeramy Thorn would later be the last elected President of the country once known as the United States of America.*

The Ship

Almost as soon as the light showed up on Ian McPherson's panel, Captain Smith was on the intercom.

"Mr. McPherson," spoke the captain, "I see a light on the engineering panel. What's happening down there?"

"Aye, captain," replied McPherson, "it looks to be that number two heat exchanger. She's been sort of twitchy since we left Southampton. I think it's time to scrap that piece of bilge and replace it with a new one."

The Captain replied, "Good idea Mr. McPherson. How long until it's fixed? You know that the first-class guests can't have cooled air or ice in their drinks until that heat exchanger is replaced."

"About three hours," replied McPherson, "and we're going to have to reduce speed by one quarter because we have to bring the temperature of number two boiler down so the men can tolerate the heat."

The captain sighed dejectedly. "Very well, make it so."

"OK lads!" said McPherson to his crew. "That number two heat exchanger is on the outs again. I told the captain that we would have that it replaced in three hours. But I know that we can do it in two hours if we really get on it.

"Donnelly, you and Connor go to cargo bay six and bring back a new heat exchanger," ordered McPherson. He turned to the Boiler Master and said, "Mr. Tillison, we need you and your crew to reduce the heat in the number two boiler by at least one hundred degrees — without dousing the entire heater. I want to be able to tell the captain that he'll have full power when we've switched out the parts."

Tillison waved in assent and quickly gathered his men, told them their assignments and then dispersed them to their various jobs.

Two hours and twelve minutes later McPherson called up to the bridge. "Captain, we've swapped out the heat exchanger and number two boiler is at capacity. Full power at your discretion, sir."

"Excellent!," beamed the captain. "Could you

give me twenty knots?"

"Aye, sir...and maybe a wee bit more," replied McPherson cheerfully.

Captain Smith noted the thrum of the great engines as the ship surged forward. Because of the prolonged time they were at reduced power, he had altered their course northward by twelve degrees. That would cut three, maybe four hours from their travel time. He was determined to beat the best time for an Atlantic crossing for a ship this size. He checked all the stations on the bridge and then went to mingle with the guests (not his favorite task), have some dinner in his cabin, and then go to bed.

At eleven-forty p.m. the loud klaxons woke the captain from his slumber. He immediately noticed that the ship was listing to starboard (right) and they were hardly moving. He called the bridge.

"Mr. Madison," inquired the captain, "what's happening up there?"

Madison shakily replied, "I think we've run aground, sir!"

"That's impossible," roared the captain. "We're over twelve hundred miles from land." He paused then said, "Tell the engine room 'All Stop' and I'll be right up."

On the way to the bridge he stopped at Thomas Andrews' room to inform the ship's designer that there was a problem and to meet him in Engineering in five minutes.

Once on the bridge, he was able to assess the extent of the problem. To say he was alarmed would have been an understatement. He issued orders to the crew and his second in command, and then headed to the engine room.

McPherson met the captain and Andrews at the door to Engineering.

"How bad, Ian?" inquired the captain.

"Bad enough," replied McPherson. "We ran into an ice hill. It made a gash in the hull that runs from cargo bay two through cargo bay seven. We're taking on water at fifteen thousand gallons an hour. I've got the boys back there with the pumps, but I don't think that the pumps can handle that amount of water."

He looked up sadly to the captain, "We lost sixteen men down there when the watertight doors slammed shut. They were good lads, each and every one of them," McPherson said.

"We'll mourn later," spoke the captain sympathetically. "But for right now we have to see if the ship is savable."

He turned to Andrews and asked, "Thomas, how many cargo compartments can flood and still have us stay afloat?"

Andrews seemed dazed but finally responded slowly, "Three, maybe four. If more than that get flooded, she goes down."

Captain Edward Smith made his decisions quickly. "Mr. McPherson, do the best that you can. But if you see it's hopeless, get you and your crew to the lifeboats. Mr. Thomas, you're with me." He pivoted quickly and made for the bridge.

Once on the bridge, he barked out orders to the crew. "Get the lifeboats ready to launch. Women and children first." There were more than two thousand people on board and they had twenty lifeboats. The ship had been designed with sixty-four lifeboats, but the owners had decided that it was 'ascetically unacceptable' to have that many lifeboats crowding the decks. And besides, they had been assured by the builders that the ship was unsinkable.

On the night of April 14, 1912, the brave

vessel was dashed all to pieces and more than one thousand helpless souls within her drowned. An additional five hundred jumped overboard into the frigid Atlantic. Those who survived the jump from the ship and who didn't drown immediately, had the heat sucked out of them by the bitterly cold water and died of hypothermia within minutes.

In the lifeboats, the crews pulled hard on the oars to give some distance from the sinking ship's pull. It was two a.m. when those in the lifeboats heard the boilers explode and saw the ship's lights go out. Twenty minutes later the ship broke apart and quickly descended to the murky deep some twelve thousand feet below.

The Cunard liner, Carpathia, arrived on the scene two hours later. Of the twenty-two hundred and twenty-four passengers aboard, only seven hundred and five, whose souls were greater than the ocean and whose spirit stronger than the seas embrace — only seven hundred and five — survived the maiden voyage of the largest ship ever built — the unsinkable RMS Titanic.

The Deal of the Century

The men met at the borrowed Consul's office in San Francisco. They were, to use a modern word, 'frenemies.' That is to say, they were on different sides of the political spectrum and both represented their respective counties with great passion and vigor and would give almost no quarter. But apart from 'work' they admired and respected each other.

The secretary opened the office door and Eduard walked in and immediately offered his hand to William.

"Mr. Secretary, how good it is to see you again," said Eduard.

"Minister," replied William, "it's always good to see you."

They shook hands and sat across from each other around the big desk.

"Well Eduard," started William, "now that all the formalities are taken care of, can I get you something to drink? Some tea perhaps? Or maybe, as

I've heard, you've started drinking coffee. Can I get you a cup of that?"

"I've tried your American coffee, but it's very bitter," spoke Eduard.

"I know what you mean," said William, "but if you add a spoon of sugar and a dash of cream, it makes the brew more tolerable."

"Really?" replied Eduard. "I would like to try coffee that way."

William rose and went to the secretary with instructions for two cups of coffee along with cream and sugar for both.

When he came back to the desk William asked, "So hows Elisa?"

"Well, when we first were moved here from Moscow, I didn't think my wife would ever adapt," replied Eduard. "But now she's made some friends, she found a good butcher, and an equally good seamstress, and I believe she's beginning to settle in."

Changing topics Eduard asked, "So what's this I hear about your son Augustus being appointed to the Military Academy? You and Frances must be very proud."

"We are!" exclaimed William. "Frankly, and

confidentially, I never thought he'd make it in. But he worked really hard, and if he keeps it up, he'll earn his commission in another two years."

They stopped chatting when the secretary entered with a tray of two cups of steaming hot coffee, a sugar bowl, a small pitcher of milk, a pair of napkins, and a small plate of cookies.

"Ah, here we are," remarked William. "Thank you, Madeline."

They sat in silence and drank their coffee and then Eduard remarked, "You're right! It is better with cream and sugar. I might get to like this even better than tea!"

After a few more moments, they both realized that it was time to get down to the serious business at hand.

"So, Eduard, what's this I'm hearing about Russia wanting to sell its interest in Russian America?" asked William.

"It's like this," began Eduard. "As I'm sure you understand, the cost of the war in the Crimea, much like your recent war, was exceptionally expensive. And, contrary to popular belief, the Tsar is not made of money!"

He paused to sip some coffee and then continued.

"Currently, there are about eleven thousand Russians who live in that vast wilderness. Mostly they hunt for skins or are loggers. And the costs of shipping goods from Russian America to the Motherland and then to Moscow is getting more costly every year.

"What can the United States do to help our Russian friends?" asked William cautiously.

"I believe," said Eduard slowly, "that the Tsar would be very grateful if the United States would enter into a treaty with Russian to purchase Russian America."

"That's a fair amount of land," said William. "a bit over three hundred seventy-five thousand acres...if I understand what my surveyors have been telling me."

"That sounds about right," replied Eduard. "But the Tsar is willing to offer you 'such a bargain'..."

Here he paused and looked hopefully to his friend.

"I know all about Russian bargains," smiled

William. But what William wasn't telling his fellow negotiator was that his government had already telegraphed him and authorized him to spend up to eight million dollars to buy the land from the Russians.

"And there's another advantage if we sell you the land," Eduard said enthusiastically. "If you own the land, then the British can't take it over and attack your western frontier from the north."

William wanted to appear that he was 'playing hard to get' so he paused as if to ponder what the deal might be.

Finally he spoke jovially. "So what's this great deal, this incredible bargain, that the Tsar has in store for us?"

He looked at William with anticipation. Eduard took a deep breath and answered, "His Excellency the Tsar of All Russia would be happy to offer you all the land in what we now call Russian America for two point six of your pennies per acre or ten million U.S. dollars."

"That's an awful lot of money Eduard," said William. "But I'm afraid that my government has only authorized me to pay up to five million.

"Five million!" said Eduard, aghast. "We both know that the resources alone are worth three times that amount."

"Yes," countered William, "but it's thirty-one hundred miles north of San Fransisco! Almost three weeks by schooner."

And so the dance began. Thrust and parry. Parry and thrust. At one point, late in the afternoon, William suggested that Eduard telegraph his government, which he did, to see if they would be amenable to lowering the price. Since it would take several hours for the message to be delivered and acted upon, the men broke for dinner and continued their earlier conversations about their families, upcoming events, births, deaths, and other types of gossip.

About ten p.m. the message was returned from Russia and the men returned to the bargaining table.

The Russians tried to sweeten the pot by agreeing to remove and relocate all Russian nationals at no cost to the U.S. The U.S. tried to get a lower price by insisting that they be given trade allowances that included discounted goods due to the distances from the mainland.

They went back and forth for many hours but finally at two a.m. on Saturday March 30th, they came to an agreement. The United States would agree to pay the Tsar of Russia one point nine cents per acre or seven point two million U.S. dollars. They sealed the deal with a glass of vodka for Eduard and a glass of fine bourbon for William. They agreed that the United States would officially take possession of Russian America on October 18, 1867.

"What are you going to call your new land?" asked Eduard. "I mean you can't keep calling it 'Russian America."

William replied, "The general consensus is that we call it what the natives call it. It's named after one of their tribes. They call it 'Alaska.'

Afterward — Secretary of State William Seward went to bed that night with high hopes for the land that would almost double the size of the United States. Unfortunately, not many on the East Coast thought so highly of this 'bargain' that the U.S. had struck with Russia, and for years afterward the 'deal of the century' was known as 'Seward's Folly.' But in the long run, as we all now know, Seward was right!

Tilich

'Rich Man, Poor Man,
Beggar Man, Thief,
Doctor, Lawyer, Indian Chief'

At one point in his six century existence, Tilich had been all of the above. But now he was to do something different. Bizarre. Unexpected. He once thought there was NOTHING new under the sun — he was wrong on that one. He used to think that there was NOTHING he hadn't tried at one point or another in his long life — he was wrong on that one, too. And he used to say there were things he'd NEVER do. And he was...well you know the answer to that one.

The two men met in an out-of-the-way bar. They sat in a booth near the back of the dark establishment. They ordered drinks and sat listening to the music and not talking until after the waitress brought their drinks.

"You come highly recommend Mr., Umm. What shall I call you?" asked the older man.

"Tilich," replied the other.

"Well, Mr. Tilich..."

He was stopped immediately by Tilich. "No Mister. Just Tilich."

"OK," replied the other gentleman. "I am L'Vod of Sandival. I am told that you are a man that can fix certain problems."

"What I can do for you, L'Vod?" asked Tilich.

L'Vod replied, "My world, Sandival, has been at war with our neighboring planet called Nafgal, for the past two centuries." He paused and then continued, "I represent a large group of businessmen and prominent citizens who want to see a permanent end to all hostilities between our worlds."

"Have you tried to sue for peace?" asked Tilich.

"For the past fifty years, we have sent peace envoys to their world — all of which have been summarily dismissed. But in their defense, they have sent envoys to us which have also been summarily dismissed," replied L'Vod.

"So what would you have *me* do?" asked Tilich

"My people are tired of war, all the costs, all the suffering," L'Vod said. "I...we want it to end forever. We don't want the Nafgali to ever be capable to ever attack us again. It doesn't matter what it costs or what measures have to be taken even if that means wiping out the Nafgali. Oh, and we want to leave the planetary infrastructure intact."

"Let me do some research and I'll get back to you on whether I'll take the job or not," commented Tilich.

Over the ensuing twenty some-odd months, Tilich did extensive research on how to destroy a planet without actually 'destroying a planet.' Both planets, Nafgal and Sandival, had similar levels of technology. Their spacecraft were similar in design and had similar capabilities. They both had invented and deployed forcefields to protect the bulk of their planets from space-based bombardment. Even their weapons of mass destruction were very similar. Tilich was amazed that there were so many similarities. So he started to dig a bit deeper. What he found was startling.

Two and a half years later the men met at the same bar.

"I have, Mr. Prime Minister," said Tilich carefully, "a solution to your problem."

L'Vod looked up quickly and replied, "So you know who I am. It doesn't matter or change the circumstances. We are desperate! Tell me what you can do for my world and what will it cost."

Tilich looked directly into the eyes of the Prime Minister and said, "I will prevent the Nafgali from ever waging war against your planet and, as you requested, leave the infrastructure of the planet intact. And, as to the cost — I believe that your government is spending about six hundred billion per year for defense. I will completely obliterate the Nafgali, every man, every woman, and every child, for two hundred million."

L'Vod looked up slowly and said quietly, "And if we accept your terms?"

"You will deposit fifty million into these banks and accounts within twenty days," said Tilich passing L'Vod a slip of paper with the bank's information.

"When I deploy, you will deposit one hundred million into the banks and accounts I designate. And when the job is completed, you will deposit the remaining fifty million into the banks and accounts I choose," ordered Tilich

"And if we are unhappy with the results?" asked L'Vod.

"You have my unconditional guarantee," said Tilich. "If, you are not satisfied with the results of my work, I will refund all of the money — minus what I will spend for research and development — and we'll part as friends."

L'Vod nodded ever so slightly and then left the table without saying a word. Tilich hoped, at least internally, that the Sandivalis would reject his offer.

And so it was some sixteen days later that Tilich was notified by the five banks on five different worlds he had designated that deposits of ten million had been deposited into each. Tilich sighed and then started making lists of what he would need to do the job.

•••

"A1 Chopper Service," said a female voice on the phone.

"Yes, hello, this is Martin Lugo," said Tilich. "My mother recently passed away and her last request was that I spread her ashes over the city where she lived all of her life. Could you help me with that? And what would the cost be?"

The woman was very sympathetic, "Yes, of course, Mr. Lugo. We would be happy to fulfill your mother's last request."

She quoted a price that was very reasonable and Tilich accepted. In all, Tilich used the same ruse in four other large cities on Nafgal.

Tilich sent a message to L'Vod, "I have deployed. You can now make the second deposits to the institutions listed below."

Four years later, Tilich and L'Vod met in a similar bar on Sandival.

Tilich began, "I deployed four years ago but I wanted to see the results before I contacted you.

"My government was beginning to..." started L'Vod.

Tilich held up his hand to interrupt, "Yes, I understand, Mr. Prime Minister." He paused for a moment. "I'd like you to accompany me to Nafgal to see the results of my work for yourself and have the opportunity to look your enemy in the eye before they are extinguished."

"I can't go to Nafgal," protested L'Vod. "I'll be recognized and then killed or worse!"

"Don't worry, Mr. Prime Minister," said

Tilich, "you will be in disguise. No one will recognize you. And even if they do, we'll be long gone."

So it was a few days later that L'Vod and Tilich were walking in the capital of Nafgal, and not without some trepidation on L'Vod's part. But no one seemed to know who he was and they wandered around the city for several hours unmolested. To L'Vod, Nafgal and its people looked very similar to his home world. They visited where the rich lived. They saw how the poor lived. They went to some elementary schools. And, finally, they had a meal at a restaurant and then returned to Sandival.

Before they parted, Tilich spoke to L'Vod. "I suspect that you have spies on Nafgal. Ask them to send you the enrollment data for some of those schools we visited. When you get the information, make the final deposits and then call me."

Not many days later after Tilich had received the call and the deposits, the men met, once again, in an out-of-the-way venue.

L'Vod started, "My agent on Nafgal said that the data shows enrollment dropping and then stopping over four years ago. What does that mean?"

Tilich replied, "Your charge to me was, 'you didn't want the Nafgali to ever be capable to ever attack you again and you wanted to leave the planetary infrastructure intact.' I have accomplished that."

"But how?" asked L'Vod.

"I created," answered Tilich unhappily, "a micro-organism that rendered every man, every woman, and every child on Nafgal sterile. There hasn't been a live birth in over five years. The youngest person on the planet is now almost nine years old. In a few years, the youngest will be twenty, then thirty, then forty and so on. But long before that, their economy will have collapsed. As the older generation dies off, there will be no new younger generation to replace them. Their cities will fall into disrepair. Their government, both local and national, will fail. And, ultimately, the planet will be depleted of people while leaving the infrastructure intact...as you requested.

"As time goes on," he continued, "they will not have enough men to replenish their armed forces. They won't have the manufacturing capabilities to produce weapons or the manpower to repair their military machines. The war between your planets will grind to a halt. You will have won your war. And the Nafgal will have been **annihilated.**"

L'Vod sat back and stared at Tilich in amazement. "Thank you," said L'Vod quietly nodding. He left the table without a goodbye, handshake, or any other acknowledgment.

While sitting by himself, Tilich thought back to the original research he had conducted, and how surprised he was when he discovered that the Nafgali and the Sandivali were of the same species. So what affected one would also affected the other. He neglected to share that finding with the Prime Minister. Nor did he detail the extraordinarily infectious nature of the **micro-organism** he had created. The Prime Minister has seen the results of the virus for himself while he was on Nafgal. And now he, himself, would bring those same results to Sandival.

Tilich ordered a double shot of their strongest intoxicant, drank it in one gulp and then left the bar — and ultimately, the planet.

Will These Bones Live?

Stark and his companion looked out over the plain in front of them. The heat and the sun were oppressive and Stark tried to shield his eyes to protect them. He turned slowly in a circle and as far as the eye could see, all the way to the horizon, there was nothing. Not a blade of grass...not a tree...a landmark. Nothing. There wasn't a cloud in the sky over this arid, desiccated locale. All he saw was parched land bereft of life.

"What is this place?" asked Stark.

"It is the Valley of the Spirits," replied his scaly friend. "It is where the bones of your kind come to finally rest."

"I don't understand," said Stark. "We bury our dead in the ground in coffins all around the world."

"Yes," replied the companion, "you do. And slowly, year by year, decade by decade, those bones are replaced by the dust that is here. Until many years later, the bones are here, and the dust is in the coffins of your loved ones."

"To what purpose?" asked Stark incredulously.

The ophidian friend continued, "They await the day when He-That-Made-All-Of-Your-Kind will bring the rain to this place and will resurrect them all."

"It's funny you said that," spoke Stark. "I had a dream last night and in it Godwin came to me and told me to speak to these bones. He said I should tell the bones: 'Thus says Godwin — I shall put sinews upon you and bring flesh upon you and draw skin over you. Then I shall put spirit into you and you shall live.'

"And in my dream," he continued, "I heard a noise while I was speaking to the bones and there was a rattling and the bones drew near, bone matching bone. Then I looked and sinews were upon them, and flesh had come up and skin had been drawn over them. Then from the four directions a spirited wind came and entered them and they stood upon their feet — a very, very vast multitude."

"He's quite mad, you know," spoke the companion. "Godwin, I mean. Ever since he lost that contest with his brother, Bruce Lawrence,

Godwin had been on a rant about how he was cheated out of his due. About how his father really wanted him to have the job and how he was going to 'take back the planet'."

"I don't understand," said Stark to his reptilian companion.

"About forty thousand of your years ago," the companion spoke, "Godwin's father decided it was time for his boys, Bruce Lawrence and Godwin, to get involved with their father's company. So their dad staked out this little planet and made a challenge to the boys. Since he didn't want them using any advanced technology or stuff like that, he said, 'Boys, you have forty thousand years to collect as many 'souls' as you can.' It was neck-and-neck for about thirty thousand years," the companion plunged on.

"Then about ten thousand years ago, Godwin started to pull ahead. In response, Bruce Lawrence hired an incredibly talented marketing manager. Year after year, century after century Bruce Lawrence pulled ahead until ten thousand years later his dad declared him the winner and gave him the job. Godwin was never the same after that."

"What can I do? What can *we* do?" inquired Stark.

"I don't know," replied Snake, sadly. "Some races, like the Overlords, are present at the birth of new planets and their species. My people are just the opposite. We are there for the final moments before the species or planet expires. It is our unhappy fate," he sighed.

"So that's it then?" questioned Stark.

"As many of your holy books foretold there would come a time when a great war would erupt — an apocalypse — a time when all Mankind, as well as the planet, would perish," the ophidian said. "Godwin hopes by bringing that time nigh he can defeat Bruce Lawrence and claim, what he believes is his rightful place at his father's side. And as you saw in your prophetic vision, Godwin will raise a vast army to try to triumph over Bruce Lawrence, and in the process, destroy both Man and the planet."

"Is there nothing that can be done? An appeal to...Someone? Something? Anything?" pleaded Stark.

The saurian shook his head, no.

During the time they had been speaking, the sun had started to descend toward the horizon. The temperature had begun to drop and then a clap of thunder was heard. Stark looked upward, saw the clouds start to form above him as the rain began to fall on the valley.

The war had begun.

Evening Prayer

Thank you, Lord, for watching over me. For protecting me. For guiding me. For shielding me. For sheltering me. For saving me.

Thank you for sending complete healing for all my ailments both large and small.

Thank you for sending complete healing to my wife, our children and their families, my brother and his wife and their entire family, to the ill Rabbis, and to all our sickened friends.

Thank you for all the food you sent me yesterday, today, and tomorrow. Every day. Every hour of every day.

Thank you for all the work you send me (and I could always use more), and thank you for the inspiration to write new stories and the continued success of my books.

Thank you for all the things you do for me which I know about, like gravity, and for all the things I don't know about.

Remember Me

This occurred many years ago...before the virus that killed my world happened. Before my parents became the catalyst for the spread of that virus. I was just a boy then...perhaps seven or eight years old.

My world, Nafgal, had been at war with our neighboring planet, Sandival, for more than two centuries. The reasons for the war have been lost but, as in most things of this nature, it was probably due to some small slight that one person in one administration made about some other person in another administration. Tempers flared and no apology was ever forthcoming and so war began.

Or it could have been about the mining rights to the asteroids that separated our planets. Or about a trade dispute. Or any number of a thousand other matters.

Both of our planets, Nafgal and Sandival, had similar levels of technology. Our spacecraft were of a similar design and had similar capabilities. We both had invented and deployed forcefields to protect the bulk of our planets from space-based bombardment. Even our weapons of mass destruction were very similar. But it wasn't until the then Prime Minister of Sandival, a man named L'Vod, and his administration had decided to completely annihilate **my planet**, that the nature and tide of the war changed.

They brought in a man that my parents knew as Martin Lugo, but whose real name was Tilich.

L'Vod told Tilich, "My people are tired of war, all the costs, all the suffering. We don't want the Nafgali to ever be capable to ever attack us again. It doesn't matter what it costs or what measures have to be taken even if that means wiping out the Nafgali. Oh, and we want to leave the planetary infrastructure intact."

Tilich, eventually and unenthusiastically, accepted the commission of the Sandivalis, and a few years later my parents entered the story. At the time my Dad was a commercial chopper pilot and Mom ran the office. One day they received a call:

"A1 Chopper Service," said Mom.

"Yes, hello, this is Martin Lugo," said Tilich. "My mother recently passed away and her last request was that I spread her ashes over the city where she lived all of her life. Could you help me with that? And what would the cost be?"

Mom was very sympathetic. "Yes, of course, Mr. Lugo. We would be happy to fulfill your mother's last request." She quoted a price that was very reasonable and Tilich accepted. In all, Tilich used the same ruse in four other large cities on Nafgal. We never knew, until later, that there was a connection between spreading her ashes over our cities and the death of my planet.

Eight years later a government report showed drop off of enrollment in elementary schools and then eventually stopping over four years later. A governmental task force was set up to study the matter to see if this drop in enrollment was happening in only a few cities or over the entire planet. That was the first hint that something was terribly wrong with my planet...and everything led back to Tilich!

Ultimately, the connection became all too clear. Tilich, as we found out, had been charged by the Sandivalis to 'make Nafgal incapable of ever attacking the Sandivalis again and they wanted to leave the planetary infrastructure intact.' How did one man do this? How does one man kill and entire planet? He created a micro-organism, a virus, that rendered every man, every woman, and every child on Nafgal sterile.

By the time we uncovered this plot, there hadn't been a live birth on Nafgal in over five years. The youngest person on the planet was then almost nine years old. A few years later, the youngest was twenty, then thirty, then forty and so on. But long before that, our economy hovered on the brink of collapse. As the older generation died off, there was no new younger generation to replace them. Our cities fell into disrepair. Our government, both local and national, started to fail.

As time went on, we did not have enough men to replenish our armed forces. We didn't have the manufacturing capabilities to produce weapons or the manpower to repair our military machines. The war between our planets moved more and more slowly and then came to a halt. But, by then, my people had been annihilated.

I am now in the twilight of my eightieth year and I am one of the youngest people alive. We were once a world of billions. Now we are a world of thousands.

Remember me. Remember what happened to Nafgal. Tell your children and your children's children so this never happens to another world.

Willing Suspension of Disbelief

I am part of an Orthodox Jewish community that holds that the Torah (the Five Books of Moses) and the Talmud (the Oral Law) were taught to Moses over the course of forty days while he stood atop Mt. Sinai while he was ninety-years-old. They believe that G-d, Himself, schooled Moses.

Call me a 'Doubting Thomas' but I find it hard to believe that a ninety-year-old man, albeit an incredible man, could memorize the almost eighty thousand words of the Torah and the one million four hundred fifty thousand words of the Talmud in just forty days. Most people I know would have a hard time memorizing the second verse of the *Star Spangled Banner* or learning the thirty thousand words of Shakespeare's *Hamlet* in a far longer time frame.

Added to this is their absolute belief that EVERYTHING written in those books is the unwavering and unalterable absolute truth. They are taught to accept that laws written thirty-three hundred years ago by a bronze-age, agrarian society are still relevant today. Really?

Case in point — Observant Jews do not drive their vehicles on the Sabbath. Why? Because within the fourth of the Ten Commandments, *Remember the sabbath day and keep it holy,* is embedded prohibitions about working on the Sabbath: "You shouldn't work, nor your wife, nor your children, man servant, maid servant, guests, or your animals." Notwithstanding that the Torah never defines what 'work' means (it IS explained in excruciating detail in the Talmud), there's still no mention of not driving. So how do we get to a prohibition of driving on the Sabbath?

Believe it or not, there were no cars **thirty-three hundred years ago.** To go to market or your neighbor's house, you had to get the horse or donkey out of the barn and hitch it up to the wagon. Then the animal would have to pull the wagon and its contents to the desired destination. That entailed work on both your part and the part of the animal. Work that the Talmud explained was not allowed on the Sabbath.

But let's face it, not many people today are hooking up their Toyotas to a mule or a donkey —

we put the key into the ignition, turn the key (or press the button) and off we go. So how does that get up to not driving on the Sabbath?

Here the rabbis fall back on another Sabbath prohibition: You are forbidden to create a fire on the Sabbath.

But wait I hear you say, there's no fire in my car. But there is! The spark plugs creates a fire that ignites the gasoline in the engine's combustion chamber. So we have 'evolved' *vis-à-vis* from the concept of working on the Sabbath prohibited due to breaking of the rules of work, to the prohibition due to creating a fire. The rules in regard to electric lights follow the same trajectory. And electric cars? Let's not go there, yet!

And it not just Observant Jews who have these issues. Both the Orthodox Muslims and various Orthodox Christian/Catholic groups are facing the same problems — How do you reconcile a belief system and worldview that was created over **thirty-three hundred years ago** years ago with contemporary American society?

Modernity is a problem for all the Abrahamic religions. So what to do? You *could* just ignore the problem. Or you *could* follow the laws as best as you can. Or you *could* say, "This is what G-d wants me to do to be a good (insert your religion here). Or there'a a fourth choice — Willing Suspension of Disbelief.

While I was at college, John Lahr (the son of Burt Lahr, 'the Cowardly Lion from *Wizard of Oz*') introduced and explained the concept of a "Willing Suspension of Disbelief."

We *know* when we go to a movie or a play that the people on stage or the screen are just actors saying lines that someone wrote for them to say. We *know* that most people don't spontaneously break out into song and dance. We *know* that good doesn't always triumph over evil. We know that! But for those two or three hours we are willing to suspend our disbelief and believe that all those people on stage and screen are as real as you or me.

Humphrey Bogart isn't Humphrey Bogart the actor, he's Rick the expat bar owner and anti-hero in *Casablanca.* Judy Garland isn't Judy Garland, the actor, she's Dorothy a pre-WWII child living in Kansas who get's swept away to Oz. And Tom Hanks isn't Tom Hanks the actor, he's Mr. Rogers in his beautiful neighborhood.

So what's an observant person to do? This is what I do. For the times I spend in synagogue or studying at the Hebrew school or engaging in lively discussions with fellow observant Jews or even, in these coronavirus times, praying virtually at home, I willingly suspend my disbelief that some of the laws and precepts written over three thousand years ago are hopelessly out of date and not realistic in the face of modernity. In other words, within that sphere, I believe. Outside of that sphere, I still believe, but somewhat differently. Will I drive on the Sabbath? No! Will I switch on a light if necessary? Yes. Did I remove the lightbulb from my refrigerator? No. Will I cook from Friday at sunset until Saturday at sunset? Nope. And there are other laws I bend. This works for me.

Will it work for other Jews? That remains to be seen. But with all the **attrition** that contemporary American Jewish communities have seen over the past few decades, we must find ways to reach out to younger and dispossessed Jews and get them back into the fold.

One way that a Dallas Jewish Outreach group

that caters to a younger crowd uses is having a 'happy hour' before worship begins on the Sabbath. A Conservative synagogue has a 'nosh' (snack) before their service begins on Friday night to tide their congregants over until they can get home to eat their Sabbath meal.

And perhaps slightly bending the rules and not adhering to 'absolute truths' might be yet another one of those ways. In truth — time will tell.

Storytelling 101

"Most people," intoned the professor, "couldn't tell a story if their lives depended on it. They either can't get the facts of the story correct or perhaps worse. They add so much superfluous claptrap that the gist of the story gets lost!"

"For example," he continued, "take this little six-line short story..." He turned to the chalkboard and scribbled:

Jack and Jill
Went up the hill
To fetch a pail of water.
Jack fell down
And broke his crown,
And Jill came tumbling after.

Turning back to his students the professor resumed. "As you can see, this story is from the Sargent Joe Friday/Dragnet school of storytelling — 'Just the facts ma'am, nothing but the facts.'

A student raised his hand and asked a question, "But professor shouldn't a story tell the facts?"

"Sure," replied the professor, "If you're

reading a story on CNN or the late-night news. But shockingly that's not what we're talking about here. Before we turn to what we're about here, let's ask some questions about Jack and Jill."

Beckoning to the class, he turned back to the chalkboard and began to write the questions that the class was hurling at him:

Who were Jack and Jill?
Why did they have go up a hill to get water?
What were the circumstances of Jack's accident?
Was 9-1-1 called to treat Jack's injuries?
Why did Jill come tumbling after?
Was she pushed or was it merely another accident?
Were there signs posted about 'being careful about falling off the hill'?
Were there other people on that hill?

This went on for many minutes. After most of the questions were posted, the professor turned to the class and began again.

"Those are good questions but also remember that the 'tone' of the story can change the answers to those questions and how the story is perceived by the reader. For example *The National Inquirer!* As he waved his hand from left to right above his head, he read the imaginary headline in a bold voice, "THE

REAL REASON JACK AND JILL WENT UP THE HILL. It Will Shock You!"

After the laughter had died down, he continued, "Or perhaps, William Shakespeare —

'A pair of star-crossed lovers, Jack and Jill,
climbing upon a hilly slope,
take their life,
Whose shocking misadventure deemed unnecessary
Doth with their death bury their strife.'

In the ensuing silence he spoke again, "Or maybe something a bit more modern...

'It was just another day in our little Shangri-La of Los Angeles. The sun was out, the beaches were full of partying people ending their quarantines, and Jack decided to head to Louie's to have a beer to celebrate. After a couple of beers, he noticed a chick sitting alone at the other end of the bar. He motioned to Sandy, the bartender, to send over whatever the chick was drinking compliments of himself. He watched the exchange and then went back to his beer and only slightly listened to the TV.

A while later the chick sat down on the barstool next to Jack.
"Hey," she said, "thanks for the drink. I'm Jill."
Jack gave her a closer look and replied, "No prob. I'm Jack. You come here often?"
She replied, "Actually, my first time. You?"

233

I've been coming to Louie's since its heyday. Back then it had dark, rich mahogany walls studded with pictures of Louie's famous customers — stars of the silver screen and Broadway, kings and potentates, congressmen, a president or two, and even the Pope all came to Louie's. Not like this..." he said looking around and gesturing to encompass the room. He dropped his hand in sorrow.

They sat and drank in silence for a bit then Jack asked, "Hey, you wanna go for a ride? I've got my bike outside. We could stop and pick up a six-pack and head up into the hills. If you've never seen LA at night from the Hollywood sign, it's breathtaking. It shocks a lot of people."

She gave him that look that women give men as she pondered the question, 'Is this a nice guy or am I considering going out with a Jack the Ripper?' She decided that Jack was a nice guy. After all, he DID buy her a drink. "Sure, let's do it," she responded.

They got up, Jack paid the bar tab, and they left together. Less than a mile from the bar was a package store. Jack hopped off the bike, went inside, and returned a short time later with the beer and a bag of ice. Before she could even ask, Jack answered with a smile, "Because I don't like *warm beer!" He put the beer and the ice into one of the saddlebags on the bike.*

They headed south along the Coastal Highway. The Pacific to their right and oncoming traffic to their left. Coming around a curve, they never saw the eighteen-wheeler that had swerved to avoid a broken-down car in the middle of the northbound lanes. The bike and its riders tumbled over the eight- hundred-foot cliff. Jack was the first to the bottom with Jill closely following. The coroner later wrote that the cause of death was massive injuries to the head.

The professor continued, "When I was a bit younger, actually way younger, I used to go up into the hills and look out upon the blossoming Los Angeles. And there was a time that I took a female friend, actually a new acquaintance, up to the 'Hollywood' sign to show her the majesty of LA. Unfortunately, that liaison didn't end well. But that was OK because her sister had a friend who knew my brother (who introduced the friend of the sister to me) and we were friends for years."

The professor awoke from his revery and continued, "Ugh, right. Where were we? Um, storytelling. That's right. So as I was saying, most people couldn't tell a great story if their lives depended on it."

Changing subjects he continued, "You know, I just remembered that there was this incredible storyteller that I met in Mumbai. A beggar actually. But he would weave the most outstanding tales, and just when he was about to reveal the killer or come to the denouement or add some salient point he would pause...waiting for someone, one of the listeners, to drop a coin or two into his bowl. He was quite extraordinary.

"Now what was I talking about?" asked the professor (more to himself than to the class). "Oh yes, storytelling!" Glancing at his watch, "Well, I seem to have gone on a bit. But the point here is try to tell the story as concisely as you can, adding any details that you feel are necessary, and a few twists to the plot wouldn't hurt either.

That'll be it for today. Sorry I went on so long. For next time, read Chapter two in Scoldby and Ross's *Guide to Storytelling.*"

How a normal person tells a story

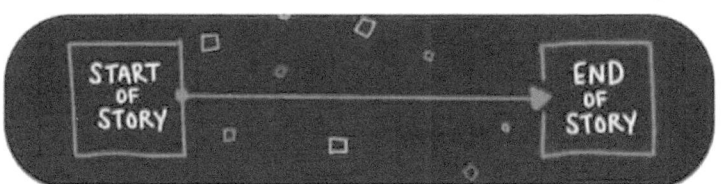

How I tell a story

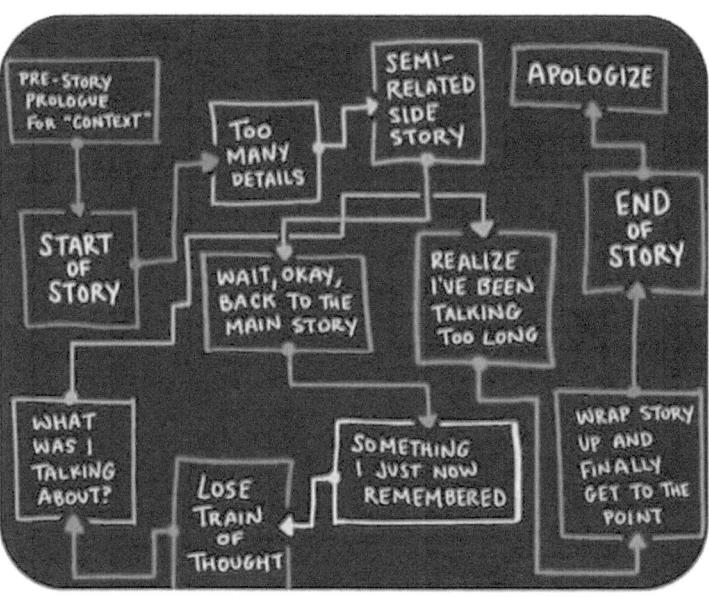

The Terrible Conflagration Up at The Place

Adapted for stage from a short story by Ray Bradbury

Time: 1914, Winter, Six p.m.
Place: Lord Kilgotten's Place in Ireland

Cast:
Riordan
Casey
Kelley
Nolan
Timulty
Murphy
Brannahan
Rooney
Blinky Watts
Tuohy
Flannery
Hannahan
Bob
Tim
Lord Kilgotten
Lady Kilgotten

(The men have been hiding down by the gatekeeper's lodge for half an hour or so passing a bottle between them. They dodge up the path at six in the evening and look at the great house)

RIORDAN

That's The Place!

CASEY

Hell, what do you mean, 'that's The Place?' We seen it all our lives.

KELLY

Sure, but with the Troubles over and around us, sudden-like The Place looks different. It's quite a toy, lying there in the snow...(to Casey) Did you bring the matches?

CASEY

Did I bring the — what do think I am?

KELLY

Well, *did* you, is all I ask.

CASEY

(Searches his pockets, can't find the matches, swears under his breath) I did not.

NOLAN

Ah, what the hell. They'll have matches inside. We'll borrow a few. Come on. (Timulty trips and falls) For G-d's sake, Timulty, where's your sense of romance? In the midst of the big Easter Rebellion, we want to do everything just so. Years from now we want to go into the pub and tell about the terrible conflagration up at The Place, do we not? If it's all mucked up with the sight of you landing on your ass in the snow, that makes no fit picture of the Rebellion we are now in, does it?

TIMULTY

(Rising and nodding) I'll mind me manners.

RIORDAN

Psst. Here we are!

CASEY

Jesus, stop saying things like, 'that's The Place' and 'here we are.' We see the damn house. Now what do we do?

MURPHY

Destroy it?

CASEY

Gah, you're so dumb you're hideous. Of course we destroy it, but first...blueprints and plans.

MURPHY

It seemed so simple enough back at Hickey's Pub. We would just come tear the damned Place down. Seeing as how my wife outweighs me, I need to tear down something!

TIMULTY

(Drinking from the bottle) It seems to me we go rap on the door and ask permission.

MURPHY

Permission? I'd hate to have you running Hell, the lost souls would never get fried We...

The front door opens and a man stares out.

KILGOTTEN

I say, would you mind keeping your voices down? The lady of the house is sleeping before we drive to Dublin for the evening and —

The men, reveled in the hearth-glow of the door, stood back, lifting their caps.

KELLY

Is that you, Lord Kilgotten?

KILGOTTEN

It is.

TIMULTY

(Smiling amicably) We will keep our voices down.

CASEY

Beg your pardon, Your Lordship.

KILGOTTEN

Kind of you. (Closes door)

CASEY

'Beg your pardon, Your Lordship,' 'we'll keep our voices down, Your Lordship.' (Slapping his head) What are we saying? Why didn't someone catch the door while he was still there?

MURPHY

We was dumbfounded, that's why...he took us by surprise just like them high and mighties. I mean, we weren't *doing* anything out here, were we?

TIMULTY

Our voices *were* a bit high.

CASEY

Voices, hell! The damned lord has come and gone from our fell clutches.

TIMULTY

Shhh...not so loud.

CASEY

(Lowering his voice) So, let's sneak up on the door and —

NOLAN

That strikes me as unnecessary, he *knows* we're here now.

CASEY

Sneak up on the door...and batter it down.

KILGOTTEN

(Peering by the door) I say, what *are* you doing out there?

CASEY

Well, it's this way, Your Lordship...

MURPHY

(Blurting out) We come...we come...to burn The Place.

KILGOTTEN

(He stands for a moment looking at the men, with his hand on the doorknob. He shuts his eyes for a moment then...) Hmmm, well in that case, you had best come in.

MEN

Fine! Great! Good! Good enough! (They all start in)

CASEY

Wait! (To Kilgotten) We'll come in when we're good and ready!

KILGOTTEN

Very well. I shall leave the door ajar and when you have decided the time, enter. I shall be in the library.

TIMULTY

(As soon as Kilgotten turns) When we are *ready*? Jesus, G-d, when will be readier? Out of the way, Casey.

They all run up on the porch. Hearing this, His Lordship turns and looks at them and says...

KILGOTTEN

Scrape your feet, please gentlemen.

TIMULTY

Scraped they are. (All the men scrape the snow and mud from their feet)

KILGOTTEN

This way, gentlemen. I will get you all a drink, and we shall see what we can do about your...how did you put it...burning The Place?

TIMULTY

You're sweet reason itself.

Kilgotten leads the men into the library, where he pours a round of whisky.

KILGOTTEN

Gentlemen...Drink!

CASEY

We decline!

MEN

(Ad lib) We decline?

CASEY

This is a sober thing we are doing and we must be sober for it.

RIORDAN

Who do we listen to, Casey or His Lordship?

For an answer all the men down their drinks and fall to coughing and gasping. Casey sees that this adds to their courage, so he drinks his, to catch up. Kilgotten, sitting and sipping his drink, is very calm.

CASEY

Your Honor, you've heard of the Troubles? I mean not just the Kaiser's War going on across the sea, but our own very great Troubles and the Rebellion that has reached even this far, to our town, our pub, and now your Place?

KILGOTTEN

An alarming amount of evidence convinces me that this is an unhappy time. I suppose what must be, must be. You have worked for me. I think I have paid you rather well on occasion.

CASEY

There's no doubt of that, Your Lordship. (Steps forward) It's just 'the old order changeth,' and we have heard of the great houses out near Tara and the great manor beyond Killashandra going up in flames to celebrate freedom and —

KILGOTTEN

(Mildly) Whose freedom? Mine? From the burden of caring for this house, which my wife and I rattle around in like dice in a cup or — well, get on. When would you like to burn The Place?

TIMULTY

If it isn't too much trouble, sir, now!

KILGOTTEN

(Sinking into his chair) Oh dear!

NOLAN

Of course, if it's inconvenient, we could come back later —

CASEY

Later? What kind of talk is *that*?

KILGOTTEN

I'm terribly sorry. Please let me explain. Lady Kilgotten is asleep now. We have some guests coming to take us to Dublin for the opening of a play by Synge...

RIORDAN

That's a damn fine writer!

NOLAN

Saw one of his plays a year ago and —

CASEY

Stand off! (The men stand back)

KILGOTTEN

We have dinner planned back here at midnight for ten people. I don't suppose you could give us until tomorrow night to get ready?

CASEY

No!

MEN

(Ad lib) Hold on! Wait a minute...

TIMULTY

Burning is one thing, but tickets is another. I mean the theatre is there, and a dire waste not to see the play, and all the food set up, it might as well be eaten. And all the guests coming. It would be hard to notify them ahead.

KILGOTTEN

Exactly what *I* was thinking!

CASEY

(Frustrated) Yes, I know. But you *don't* put off burnings. You *don't* reschedule them like tea parties, dammit, you *do* them!

RIORDAN

(Under his breath) You do if you remember to bring the matches.

NOLAN

On top of which, the Missus above is a fine lady and needs a last night of entertainment and rest.

KILGOTTEN

Very kind of you. (Refills Nolan's glass)

NOLAN

Let's take a vote!

CASEY

(Scowling around) Hell! I see the vote count already. Tomorrow night will do, dammit!

KILGOTTEN

Bless you. There will be cold cuts laid out in the
kitchen, you might want to check in there first, you
shall probably be hungry, for it will be heavy work.
Shall we say eight o'clock tomorrow night? By then I
shall have Lady Kilgotten safely to a hotel in Dublin.
I should not want her knowing until later that her
home no longer exists.

RIORDAN

G-d, you're a Christian!

KILGOTTEN

Well, let us not brood on it. I consider it past already,
and I never think of the past, gentleman.

*Kilgotten exits toward the front door with the men following
behind. Almost to the door, he stops and turns back to look
on a large portrait of an Italian nobleman. He stares for a
long time then...*

NOLAN

Your Lordship, what is it?

KILGOTTEN

I was just thinking...you love Ireland, do you not?

MEN

(Ad lib) My G-d yes! Of Course!

KILGOTTEN

Even as I do. And do you love all that is in it, in the land, in her heritage?

MEN

(Ad lib) Yes, of course. Certainly.

KILGOTTEN

I worry about things like this. This portrait is by Van Dyke. It is very old and very fine and very important and very expensive. It is, gentlemen a National Art Treasure.

MEN

(Ad lib) Is *that* what it is? It surely is! (They crowd around for a better look.)]

TIMULTY

Ah G-d, it is fine work!

NOLAN

The flesh itself.

RIORDAN

Notice how his little eyes seem to follow you around?

MEN

(Ad lib) Uncanny. Strange.

KILGOTTEN

Do you realize this Treasure, which does not truly belong to me, nor you, but to all the people as a precious heritage, this picture will be lost forever tomorrow night?

The men gasp. They hadn't realized.

TIMULTY

G-d save us, we can't have that!

RIORDAN

We'll move it out of the house first.

CASEY

Hold on!

KILGOTTEN

Thank you, but where would you put it? Out in the weather it would soon be torn to shreds by wind, dampened by rain, and flaked by hail. No, no, perhaps it is best if it burns quickly —

TIMULTY

None of that! I'll take it home myself.

KILGOTTEN

And when the great strife is over you will then deliver into the hands of the new government this precious gift of Art and Beauty from the past.

TIMULTY
Err...every single one of those things I'll do.

CASEY
(Eyeing the canvas) How much does the monster weigh?

KILGOTTEN
(Faintly) I would imagine seventy to one hundred pounds, within that range.

CASEY
Then how the hell do we get it to Timulty's house?

TIMULTY
Me and Brannahan will carry the dammed treasure and, if need be, Nolan, *you* lend a hand.

KILGOTTEN
Posterity will thank you. (He moves back down the hall. The men follow.) These are two nudes...

MEN
(Ad lib) They *are* that! Saints be praised!

KILGOTTEN
By Renoir.

ROONEY
That's the French gent that made them? If you'll excuse the expression.

MEN

(Ad lib) It looks French. That it does!

KILGOTTEN

These are worth several thousand pounds.

NOLAN

You'll get no argument from me. (He tries to touch the painting and is slapped down by Casey.)

BLINKY WATTS

I...I would like to volunteer a home for these two French ladies. I thought I might tuck those two Art Treasures, one under each arm, and hoist them to the wee cot.

KILGOTTEN

(With gratitude) Accepted. (He continues down the hall to another picture.)

ROONEY

"Twilight of the Gods?" Twilight, hell! It looks like the beginning of a great afternoon!

KILGOTTEN

I believe that there is irony in both the title and the subject. Note the glowing sky, the hideous figures hidden in the clouds. The gods are unaware, in the midst of their bacchanal, that Doom is about to descend.

BLINKY WATTS
I do not see the Church or any of her girly priests up in them clouds.

NOLAN
It was a different kind of Doom in those days. Everyone knows *that*!

FLANNERY
Me and Tuohy will carry the demon gods to my place. Right Tuohy?

TUOHY
Right!

They continue down the hall until they come to a rather grisly oil of a man, hung in a dimly lit alcove.

KILGOTTEN
Portrait of myself, done by her Ladyship. Leave it here, please.

NOLAN
You mean you want it to go up in the conflagration?

KILGOTTEN
Now, of course, if you really want to be saving...there are a dozen exquisite Ming vases in the house...

NOLAN

As good as collected.

KILGOTTEN

A Persian carpet on the landing...

NOLAN

We will roll it up and deliver it to the Dublin
museum.

KILGOTTEN

And that exquisite chandelier in the mail dining
room...

CASEY

(Tired) It shall be hidden away until the Troubles are
over.

KILGOTTEN

(Shaking each man's hand) Well then, perhaps you
might start now, don't you imagine? I mean, you do
have a largish job preserving the National Treasures.
I shall nap for five minutes before dressing. (Exits)

The men watch him leave then...

BLINKY WATTS

Casey, has it crossed your small mind, if you'd
remembered to bring the matches there would be no
such long night of work as this ahead?

CASEY

Shut up! Okay, Flannery you on the end of "Twilight of the Gods." You, Tuohy on the far end where the maid is being given what's good for here. Ha! Lift!

They carry the painting and other Art treasures outside and they are racked against each other against the house.

LADY KILGOTTEN

Where are all the paintings?

KILGOTTEN

Sent out to be cleaned. Now come along or we'll be late.

As they come out the front door, Casey and the men rush to form a mob in front of the paintings. And as the Lord and Lady leave...

MEN

(Ad lib) Good bye.

The men take the pictures away in groups of two or three. When the last one is gone Kelley goes back in to check and see if they missed anything. He stands before Lady Kilgotten's portrait of Kilgotten, shrugs and then carries the portrait into the night.

•

The clock strikes three and we find Kilgotten in the Library, among the empty walls, with a muffler around his neck, and a glass of brandy in this hand.

There is a creak, then a shift of shadows, and then cap in hand stands Casey at the Library door.

CASEY

Psst!

KILGOTTEN

(Sleepily) Oh dear me! Is it time for us to go?

CASEY

That's tomorrow night. And anyways, it's not you that's going. It's them is coming back.

KILGOTTEN

Them? Your friends?

CASEY

No, yours! (He beckons the Lord to follow him. He goes to the front door and there like demoralized solders, stand the men with their hands full of pictures, pictures leaned against their legs etc...A terrible silence lay over and among the men.)

CASEY

Is that you, Riordan?

RIORAN

And who the hell would it be?

KILGOTTEN

What do they want?

TIMULTY

It's not so much what *we* want, as what *you* might now want from *us*?

HANNAHAN

(Coming into the light) You see, considering it in all its aspects, your Honor, we've decided, you're such a fine gent, we...

BLINKY WATTS

We will *not* burn down your house!

MEN

(Ad lib) Shut up and let the man talk!

HANNAHAN

(Nodding) That's it! We will not burn down your house!

KILGOTTEN

But see here. I'm quite prepared. Everything can be easily moved out.

KELLEY

You're taking this whole thing too lightly, begging your pardon, Your Honor. Easy for you is not easy for us.

KILGOTTEN

(Not understanding) I see.

TUOHY

It seems we have, all of us, in just the last few hours, developed problems. Some to do with the home and some to do with the transportation and cartages. If you get my drift. Who'll explain first. Kelley? No? Casey? Riordan?

FLANNERY

(Sigh) It's this way —

KILGOTTEN

Yes?

FLANNERY

Well, me and Tuohy here got half through the woods, like damn fools, and was across two-thirds of the bog with this large picture of the "Twilight of the Gods," when we began to sink!

KILGOTTEN

Your strength failed?

TUOHY

Sink, Your Honor! Just plain sink into the ground!

KILGOTTEN

Dear me!

TUOHY

You can say that again, your Lordship. Why, together me and Flannery and the demon gods must have weighed close on six hundred pounds, and that bog out there is infirm if it's anything. And the more we walk the deeper we sink. And a cry strangled in me throat, for I'm thinking of those scenes in the old story where the Hound of the Baskervilles or some such fiend chases the heroine out in the moor and down she goes in a watery pit, wishing she had kept at that diet, but it's too late, and the bubbles rise to pop on the surface. All of this a-throbbing in me mind, your Honor.

KILGOTTEN

And so?

FLANNERY

And so we just walked off and left the damn gods there in their twilight.

KILGOTTEN

(A trifle upset) In the middle of the *bog*?

FLANNERY

Ah, we covered them up. I mean we put our muffler over the scene. The gods will not die twice, Your Honor. Say did you hear *that* boys? The gods...

KELLEY

Ah, shut up! Ya dimwits! Why didn't you bring the damn portrait off the bog?

TUOHY

We thought we would come get two more boys to help...

NOLAN

Two more? That's four men, plus a parcel of gods. You'd sink twice as fast...'and the bubbles rising' ya dimwits!

TUOHY

I never thought of that!

KILGOTTEN

It has been thought of now. Perhaps several of you will form a rescue team...

CASEY

It's done, Your Honor! Bob, you and Tim dash off and save the pagan deities.

BOB

You won't tell Father Leary?

CASEY

Father Leary my behind! Get! (They leave)

KILGOTTEN

(To Nolan and Kelley) I see you, too, have brought your rather large picture back.

KELLEY

At least we made it within a hundred yards of the door, sir. I suppose you're wondering *why* we have returned it, Your Honor?

KILGOTTEN

With the gathering in of coincidence upon coincidence (going to fetch his tweed cap) yes, I was given to speculate.

KELLEY

It's me back. It gave out not five hundred yards down the main road. The back has been springing out and in for five years now, and me suffering the agonies of Christ. I sneeze and fall to my knees, Your Honor.

KILGOTTEN

(Rubbing his back) I have suffered the self-same delinquency. It is as if someone had driven a spike into one's spine.

KELLEY

The agonies of Christ, as I said.

KILGOTTEN

Most understandable then that you could not finish

your journey with that heavy frame. And most commendable that you were able to struggle back this far with that dreadful weight.

KELLEY

(Standing taller and beaming) It was nothing. I'd do it again, save for the string of bones above me ass. Begging pardon, Your Honor.

Kilgotten turns toward Blinky Watts.

BLINKY WATTS

Ah, G-d, there was no trouble with sinking bogs or knocking my spine out of shape. I made it back to the house in ten minutes flat, dashed into the wee cot, and began hanging the pictures on the wall, when my wife came up behind me. Have you ever had your wife come up behind ya, Your Honor, and just stand there mum's the word?

KILGOTTEN

I seem to recall a similar circumstance.

BLINKY WATTS

Well, your Lordship, there is no silence like a woman's silence, don't you agree? And no standing there like a woman's standing there like a monument out of Stonehenge. The mean temperature dropped in the room so quick that I suffered from the polar concussions, as we call it in our house. I did not dare turn and confront the Beast or daughter of the Beast in deference to her mom. But finally, I heard her suck in a great breath and let it out very cool and calm like a Prussian general.

'That woman is a naked as a jay bird' and 'That other woman is as raw as the inside of a clam at low tide.' says she. 'But,' said I, 'these are studies in natural physique by a famous French artist.' 'Jesus-come-after-me-French' she cried, 'the-skirts-half-way-up-to-your-bum-French! The-dress-half-down-to-your-navel-French. And the gulping and smothering they do with their mouths in their dirty-novels-French and now you come home and nail French on the walls, why don't you while you're at it, pull the crucifix down and nail one fat naked lady there!'

Well, Your Honor, I just shut my eyes and wished my ears would fall off. 'Is this what you want our boys to look at last thing at night as they go to sleep?' she says. Next thing I know I'm on the path and here I am and here's the raw-oyster nudes, Your Honor, beg your pardon, thanks, much obliged.

KILGOTTEN
They *do* seem to be unclothed. I always thought of summer looking at them.

BLINKY WATTS
From your seventieth birthday on, Your Lordship, perhaps. But *before* that?

KILGOTTEN

(Lecherous) Uh, yes, yes. (His eyes drift over the crowd until they find Tim and Bob)

BOB

I got the thing all the way home and couldn't get the damn thing through the door or any window for that matter.

TIM

Well, Your Honor, I had no problem whatsoever getting it in my house. But you see, Your Lordship, it's me wife. She said we'd be the laughingstock of the town. The only family in the village with a Rubens worth half-a-million pounds and not even a cow to milk.

Kilgotten opens the door wide and the men start to file in. Kelley is the last in, and he is stopped by Kilgotten, who stares at the painting under his arm.

KILGOTTEN

My wife's portrait of me?

KELLEY

None other!

Kilgotten stares at Kelly and then at the painting, and then out toward the snowy night. Kelly smiles softly and then exits quickly with the painting. From the wings, we hear a laugh and then Kelley re-enters, empty-handed. Kilgotten shakes his hand, once. Kilgotten starts off toward the library and the men follow. Kilgotten pours them all a round of whisky.

KILGOTTEN

Well now, what shall we drink to?

FLANNERY

Why, to his Lordship, if course!

MEN

(Ad lib) His Lordship. (They all cough and sneeze, etc...)

KILGOTTEN

(Waits until all the commotion has died down) To our Ireland! (Drinks)

MEN

(Ad lib) Ah, god. Amen!

KILGOTTEN

(Looking at the picture over the hearth) I do hate to mention it — that picture...

CASEY

Sir?

KILGOTTEN

(Apologetically) It seems to be a trifle off-center, on the tilt. I was wondering if you might...

CASEY

Mightn't we boys? (All the men rush to right the picture.)

CURTAIN

The Call of the Wild Geese

"It's small things," she said to her friend Mary Pat, "things that only a wife would notice."

"Like?" inquired Mary Pat.

"Well, when I ask him where his favorite shaving mug was, he said since he stopped shaving he didn't need it anymore so he gave it to his friend, Mike, who always admired it. In and of itself not a big deal, but I gave him that mug as a birthday present.

"And then he invited me into the kitchen to help him cook!"

"And that's a big deal?" asked Mary Pat.

"MP," she continued. "I've been married to that man for going on thirty years now. Not once since we've been married has he ever let me cook. Ever! Three meals a day. Every day. Week-in and week-out for thirty years. And *now* he wants to teach me to cook?"

"Hmmm," said Mary Pat. "Anything else,

Betty Sue?"

"Well...there was the thing with his blue suit," said Betty Sue.

"His blue suit?" questioned Mary Pat.

"A few weeks ago, I was hanging his shirts in the closet and I noticed his blue suit was missing. As you probably know James Michael is not the spiffiest dresser in town. As a matter of fact, he has only three suits — A black one for funerals. The blue one and a sorta tan one. So when I ask him where the blue suit was he said that he had taken it to the cleaners. I let it go but when I went to the cleaners later that week to drop off some shirts and such, I asked about picking up James Michael's blue suit and they said they didn't have it. It'd been months since they saw it," said Betty Sue.

"Oh, my!" exclaimed Mary Pat.

"And he gave Junior his favorite pair of cuff links and his Dad's pocket watch," declared Betty Sue.

"You don't think," Mary Pat asked cautiously, "that he's having one of those 'mid-life crises' like men of a certain age get?"

"Like he wants to buy a two-seater sports car or such?" replied Betty Sue. "No, I don't think so. First of all," she continued, "we don't have the kind of money that we could afford a new — or even used — sports cars. Second of all, James Michael isn't a 'sports car' sort of guy. If anything, he'd want an RV."

"An RV?" quipped Mary Pat.

"Yeah," explained Betty Sue, "before we got married we talked about, someday, we would get an RV and travel around the U.S. About how that might soothe his wanderlust. To follow the call of the wild geese."

"To follow the call of the what?" asked Mary Pat.

"Wild geese, MP," said Betty Sue. "Haven't you ever heard that expression?"

Mary Pat admitted she hadn't.

"Ever since I met James Michael, I always got the sense that he felt tied down and that, if he had his druthers, he'd be off gallivanting around the countryside getting into trouble. But, as you know, right after we got married we had Junior and then two years later, Elizabeth Sue, and then, well you know, all the rest of the kids. But I always felt, deep down inside, that he wanted to be" — gesturing — "out there."

•••

"So what's it gonna be?" asked the friend.

"Well," said James Michael thoughtfully, "things do seem to have quieted down since all the kids are gone. And I've made sure that Betty Sue is gonna be OK, financially I mean. So 'now' might be a good time..."

"But you're not one hundred percent sure," said the friend.

James Michael mused for a moment and couldn't think a really good reason to stay...nor could he think of a really good reason to leave, now. "I need more time," he remarked.

"No problem," replied the friend, "I've got all the time in the world. I'll wait."

•••

A few weeks later Mary Pat called her friend. "Betty Sue," she said into the phone, "how's James Michael doing?"

"Oh, I don't know," groused Betty Sue. "Somedays he's fine, full of vim and vigor. But it seems like more and more he's listless. He mopes. Now I've seen this before. It's usually when he's trying to make a big decision. He'll bend himself into a pretzel trying to figure things out and when he does, he's fine again. But until then...Lawd help us!"

•••

James Michael looked up to see that his friend had returned. "I was wondering when you'd show up again."

"And?" questioned the friend.

"After weighing all the pros and cons, all the good points and bad points," said James Michael, "I have a few questions."

"Shoot," replied the friend.

Gesturing to the surroundings, "What's to become of all of this?" said James Michael.

"As you told me," said the friend patiently, "Betty Sue is gonna be taken care of financially, and I suppose that also means the kid, too."

James Michael nodded 'yes.'

"You made your will known years ago. So the lawyers can haggle about all of your stuff that you'll leave behind. But in the meantime, you'll be 'out there' free as a bird, able to follow your life's ambition to wander hither, thither and yon."

"And if I don't like it, can I come back?" James Michael questioned.

"With so much out there to discover, would you really want to? Do you think Betty Sue would have you back under those circumstances?"

"No," said James Michael, sadly, "probably not. But I would have liked to at least say good-bye."

"She'll understand, I promise" said the friend.

James Michael nodded his assent. "OK, then. Let's go!"

As they were heading out the door, James Michael could have sworn he heard the cries from above.

•••

Betty Sue's phone rang at six-fifteen a.m. She anxiously answered the phone, "Yes?"

"Mrs. Stafford? This is Doctor Babb at the hospital. I'm calling to let you know that James Michael passed away in his sleep about ten minutes ago. From the expression on his face, he seemed to finally be at peace. I'm terribly sorry. If there's anything I can do..."

Betty Sue thanked him, hung up the phone, and then slowly wandered out onto the front porch. Deep in thought she faintly heard them. Listening more closely she realized what she was hearing were geese. And as she looked up she spotted the 'flying V' formation, and she knew deep in her heart, that James Michael was finally among them.

Out Bullying
the Bullies

Fawkes, a.k.a. Matt Jeffreys, a.k.a Alex Knobel looked over his team in the meeting room.

"First, let me say before we begin, 'Thank you' to all of you for the great job we did in Baltimore. Because of our efforts, and the efforts of many others, Baltimore now has a newly elected Mayor, several Councilman, and a new Police Chief. Hopefully, we'll start to see a decrease in the targeting of black men in that city. Secondly, it's nice to be back after my forced security confinement, courtesy of the FBI, during all the trials in Maryland.

And lastly, the task before us is strikingly different than what we encountered in Baltimore. There were dealing with a corrupt city government and complicit police department. Here we're going to be up against a corrupt Federal Department of Homeland Security, a complicit President, and the mercenaries (the mercs), which they've designated as 'Federal Agents', who they've hired to incite terror and disrupt Portland's citizens free exercise of their First Amendment rights. They're playing tough. We're gonna be tougher. A lot tougher."

He paused for a second and then began in earnest —

•Alpha Team1 — Your job is to locate a space, probably a warehouse, where we can house all the players that we remove from the field of play. Think of it as a 'penalty box,' but instead of being out of the game for two minutes, they could be out of the game for, conceivably, a very long time. We'll also need food, water, sanitation, and bedding. I'm hoping it'll be less, but prepare for at least three hundred.

Alpha Team2 — Your job is to strip the players of all their gear, uniforms, and personal affects right down to their skivvies, conduct a very close inventory of all items, so they can be returned to the proper authorities at the end of this, and to make sure that the players are securely shackled to each other. This should be relatively easy since they should be unconscious. Our 'captain' will take it from there.

•Bravo Team1 — Your job is to get your drones into the air just before I confront the mercs and to track the responding police and mercenary units from their starting points and then stay with them until the end.

•Bravo Team2 — Your job is to get your drones airborne and transmitting on every available Internet channel, as well as every broadcast and narrow cast channel available, and stream this entire event in real time.

•Bravo Team3 — Your job is to protect our ground assets, namely Delta Team, with your drones by giving them adequate time to evacuate their location if you can't adequately harass the police department and mercenary forces.

•Bravo Team4 — Your job is to harass the police department and mercenary forces arial assets. Keep them busy dodging you and they won't have time to have eyes on us.

•Charlie Team — Your job is to make sure that we have uninterrupted and uninterruptible real-time communication not only between ourselves but also with data processing.

•Charlie Team2 — Your job is to interrupt

and jam all police department and mercenary forces command frequencies. Lack of 'command and control' will cripple them.

•Delta Team1 — With your laser scopes and my suggestive comments, I hope to convince the trigger-happy, baton-wielding, gas-grenade-lobbing mercs that an attack on me would be very detrimental to them. Only fire where and when and at what targets I direct you to fire at. Your weapons will be loaded with anesthezine darts. It takes about five seconds for the drug to take effect. It will render the mercs out cold for about two hours. You will also work with Alpha Team1 to install anesthezine gas jets in the holding facility...in case of emergencies.

•Delta Team2 — Your job is to have sufficient transportation and manpower available to safely and securely transport the sleeping mercs to our holding facility. Two to three people per federal agent. Throw them in the van and get gone. Ten seconds max. We'll scramble the GPS signals so you can't be tracked. And when you're done with the capture, get back to the playing field.

•Gamma Team — The Legal Beagles. You

might have the most difficult task of any of us. You get to keep us out of jail or bail us out of jail *if* we do get arrested.

And finally, Zulu Team — Like in Baltimore, you have the most important job...to look after and protect my sorry ass. Even though we have an improved individual force field generator, I don't want to take any chances that me or anyone else will get hurt out there. If this thing goes south, your job is to get me out of there, pronto.

He continued — "Over the next few days, I'll be talking to the protesters and their leaders and impressing upon them that we're here to help turn the tide in their favor and, for their safety, ask them to follow our instructions to the letter. It's imperative that we do all we can to separate the 'legitimate protesters' from the 'mostly-out-of-town rioters.' The rioters will get what they deserve...their day in court witnessing, firsthand, how the U.S. legal system works. And the protesters will get what they deserve...the Constitutional assurance of their First Amendment rights.

"And finally," Knoble noted, "let me introduce 'Chip' and 'Dale.' We have these two extraordinary gentlemen on loan from my friend and colleague, Dr. Joel Rice. They will help us coordinate and maximize all of our efforts. The mercs are expecting sheep. What they're going to get are wolves.

And so it was several days later that Knoble, replete with this iPhone set to record, and several 'leaders' from various protesting groups approached the line of soldiers on S.W. Salmon Street. As a group they stopped fifteen feet from the soldiers.

Knoble spoke slowly and clearly to the lead soldier. "Sir, I want and need to speak to your commanding officer."

The soldier glanced at Knoble and folks the with him and responded, "Move along or you'll be arrested."

"Sir," said Knoble, "with respect, I prefer to wait here to speak with your C.O. And please be advised, this encounter is being videoed by a number of drones overhead. That video is being broadcast on every available Internet channel, as well as every broadcast and narrow cast channel available, and is streaming this entire event in real time."

And quietly into his microphone he said,

"Delta Teams One and Two on hot standby."

The lead soldier took a deep breath, looked to his comrades, and almost as one, they began to advance on Knoble and his group.

Knoble shook his head and spoke into his mic, "Delta Team — Light 'em up!" He shouted to the advancing soldiers, "Gentlemen, you will notice that you all now have small red dots on strategic locations of your uniforms. People who are knowledgeable about such things, tell me that the bullets used in rifles connected to scopes that produce those red dots could blow a hole in a Kevlar™ vest about the size of a basketball. So please, be very careful. I don't want to create any widows or orphans today."

The mercenaries froze and quickly looked at themselves and then at each other. They scrambled to take much more defensive positions.

The earpiece in Knobel's right ear pinged to report that Charlie Team2 had disabled all federal agents and local police communications for a sixteen-square-block area. Bravo Team3 and Bravo Team4, also reported that they were 'on the job.'

Knoble called out to the soldiers,

"Gentlemen, you have nothing to fear from us so long as you don't make sudden moves. Perhaps if you sent the senior officer in your squad, we could chat."

Five soldiers rose slowly from the shadows and carefully approached Knobel, who hadn't moved. All five had multiple red dots on their uniforms.

"You're all under arrest," said the lead soldier looking at the group.

"On what charge?" retorted Knoble.

"Obstructing a federal agent," the soldier snapped back.

"Listen, friend," said Knoble sadly but with determination, "you're no more a Federal Agent than I am the Pope. Federal Agents don't cover their unit identification or their names. You're a mercenary. You know that, I know that, and everyone watching this video knows that."

Just then Bravo Team3 reported that there were two soldiers cautiously approaching from the east, two making their way from the west, and another two coming from the north and that it appeared that they were going to try to outflank

Knoble and his group.

Knoble wasn't having any of that. "Delta1," he spoke into his mic, "do you have eyes on the six soldiers approaching the target area?"

He received an affirmation. "Fine,"replied Knoble. "Put 'em in the penalty box." Forty seconds later Knoble heard, 'Mission accomplished' from Delta Team2.

In the minute or so that Knoble had be conversing with his teams, he had missed some of the 'conversation' with the soldier.

The soldier was shouting at Knoble, "We are duly authorized Federal Agents and if you don't move you will be forcibly arrested and charged with trespassing."

Knoble responded calmly, "This is a public street. I am not blocking traffic. My group and I intend to 'stand our ground' until we talk with your C.O."

"We'll see about that," the mercenary shouted back. He turned and briskly walked back to his squad.

Within seconds, four teargas canisters were lobbed at the protesters. The smoke enveloped the forcefield.

Fortunately Knoble and his teams had anticipated this attack. Dale altered the opacity of the forcefield and changed its color to match that of the smoke. While that was happening, an opening appeared at the back of the field away from the soldiers, and people brought in folding chairs, a card table, and lemonade for everyone. By the time the smoke had cleared, Knoble and his compatriots were sitting comfortably and chatting calmly, enjoying a glass of the sweet tart juice.

The soldiers, having expected the group to either have withdrawn or be convulsing due to the gas, were more than surprised to see the entire group sitting, unaffected, sipping a beverage. Knoble rose and spoke again to the the soldiers.

"Sir, I want and need to speak to your commanding officer." He asked Delta Team1 how many mercenaries were in this group and was answered with "Eleven." "Prepare to remove them from the playing field," was Knoble's reply.

Knoble addressed the soldier again, "Listen, Sarg, if you are incapable of getting your C.O. down here to speak to a citizen, maybe we'll have to go find him ourselves."

As the rest of Knoble's group rose and started forward, the soldiers attacked. And almost as quickly, a flight of darts from Delta Team1 found their targets and the soldiers went to sleep. Delta Team2 had them removed to the penalty box in just under ten seconds. Knoble turned to his cohorts and told them to sit back down again and relax.

"Now we wait," he said.

The waiting didn't take long. About ten minutes later, a group of nine soldiers walked confidently toward Knoble and his group and 'surrounded' their space. Since the soldiers were outside of the forcefield's fifteen-foot perimeter, they were unaware of its existence.

The lead soldier called out to Knoble, "You are ordered to move along or be forcibly detained."

Knoble, not even bothering to stand up to address the soldier, spoke into his mic, "Delta Team — Light 'em up!"

He shouted back to the advancing soldiers, "Gentlemen, you will notice that you all now have small red dots on strategic locations of your uniforms. People who are knowledgeable about such things tell me that the bullets used in rifles connected to scopes that produce those red dots could blow a hole in a Kevlar™ vest about the size of a basketball. So please, be very careful. I don't want to create any widows or orphans today."

The mercenaries froze and quickly looked at themselves and then at each other in abject surprise.

"Sir," said Knoble rising, "Please run back and tell your C.O. that a citizen requests his company to talk."

"Why should I do that, butthead?" replied the soldier.

"Because," advised Knoble, "one — you and all your men are targeted, two — your C.O. will be very angry if you don't, and three — your wasting my time is starting to piss me off. Knoble turned to his chair and lemonade.

The lead soldier gave the command for his troops to move in. They didn't take more than two steps before they joined their fellow mercenaries in the penalty box. This went on four more times. Then Delta Team1 informed Knoble that a large body of mercenaries, about forty, was advancing on their position. Knoble turned and told his group what was about to transpire and not to be alarmed or afraid. So long as they were with him they were safe.

The ersatz federal agents came to within twenty-five feet of Knoble's position and stopped. From the darkness, a lone soldier emerged. "You are ordered to move along or be forcibly detained and questioned," he spoke.

Knoble responded calmly, "This is a public street. I am not blocking traffic. My group and I intend to 'stand our ground' until we talk with your C.O."

He spoke to Delta Team1 who lit-up all the soldiers and he gave the 'small red dot' spiel, again. And, predictably, the mercenaries attacked, head on and, as before, they joined their comrades in the penalty box.

This is crazy, thought Knoble. *We're not getting anywhere here.* He informed his Teams that he was moving out and headed toward the Edith Green-Wendell Wyatt Federal Building, the location of the mercenary's headquarters.

"Delta Teams1 and 2," called Knoble, "you're about to get very busy. Anyone who looks to be an attacker and comes within six feet of the 'bubble' send them to the penalty box."

Then he told those in the bubble with him what the plan was. And so it was that they walked slowly toward S.W. Second Avenue. They made it almost to S.W. Fifth Avenue before they were accosted by a group of bellicose soldiers.

"Hey, where do you think you're going?" asked the lead soldier.

Knoble slowed his pace just long enough to say, "We have been trying to get your C.O. to speak with us for a few hours and since Mohammed won't come to the mountain..." Knoble waited for some recognition of the quote from the soldier but it wasn't forthcoming so he said, "We're going to speak with him at your HQ at the Federal Building."

"I don't think so, bub," said the soldier. "And if you proceed any further, you'll be forcibly placed under arrest and detained."

"Just try," was Knoble's reply.

They did and quickly joined the other soldiers in the penalty box. They met three more squads as they proceeded along their route. All were sent to the penalty box. And judging by the mercenary's responses, Knoble knew that Charlie Team2 was johnny-on-the-spot with their communications interruption.

When Knoble and the protester's leaders reached the intersection of S.W. Madison and S.W. Second across from the Federal Building, they stopped and waited. The Federal Building was surrounded by a ten-foot high chainlink fence topped with barbed wire and protected by one hundred fifty soldiers. Shortly, they were approached by a soldier wearing a captain's bars and in the company of his two lieutenants.

"Who the hell are you and what do you want?" asked the captain.

Knoble replied calmly, "I am Alex Knoble and these people with me are the leaders from all the protester groups. We've come to speak with your C.O. about a way to save face, save his command, and a way out of this quagmire you mercenaries have created."

"The Colonel isn't available," barked the soldier, "so you'll have to deal with me."

Just then a soldier ran up to the captain, saluted, and handed him a piece of paper. He read it and asked the soldier through clenched teeth, "What do you mean that we've lost all communications with our field troops? How many are unaccounted for?"

The soldier answered the best he could and was dismissed.

The captain turned toward Knoble and asked, "What do you know about our loss of communications with our field troops?"

"Me?" said Knoble with feigned innocence. "I'm just a citizen out for a nighttime stroll with a few of his friends. But I'm told that downtown Portland is cellphone hell."

"And our lost troops?" demanded the captain.

"Lost your troops? That can't be a good thing. Damned clumsy if you ask me," noted Knoble. "Perhaps if you roused your Colonel, he and I might be able to find a way out of this conundrum and maybe even locate your fellow mercs."

"FU!" roared the captain. He pivoted and returned to his troops.

The mercenaries brought tear gas grenades, flash grenades, batons, and their AK-47s against the unarmed, well...not so unarmed, Knoble and the protest leaders. It was as if the soldiers brought knives to a gun fight. The ensuing battle lasted all of thirty minutes and, in the end, the number of mercenaries in the penalty box grew by more than one hundred fifty. Knoble *et. al* barely had time to draw a breath before a utility truck with a crane came to a stop adjacent to the fence. They crowded into the gondola and were hoisted over the fence. They were followed by chairs, tables, food, drink, a radio, a few cots, and a porta-potty.

As soon as they were all situated, Knoble gave the command and the entire block containing the Federal Building was sealed, via an opaque force field, from the outside world. No one in. No one out. Knoble returned to his friends, sat down to dinner, and awaited the inevitable reconnoiter and encounter with the mercs.

Knoble called out to the encroaching soldiers, "Gentlemen, you have nothing to fear from us so long as you don't make sudden moves. Perhaps if you sent the senior officer in your squad to get your C.O. then we could chat."

The soldier demanded, "Put your hands up and get on your knees — you're all under arrest for trespassing on federal property."

"I don't feel like I'm under arrest," said

Knoble. Turning to those in the bubble with him, "Do any of you feel like you're under arrest?" They indicated they did not.

Knoble turned away from the soldier and returned to his dinner table. "Tell your C.O. when he is ready to talk, we'll be here waiting."

The attack came while they eating dessert. The four cameras within the bubble transmitted every detail in high resolution audio and video to the world. The soldiers tried every non-lethal weapon at their disposal. When they realized that non-lethal weapons were ineffective, they switched to lethal weapons. Also ineffective.

About ninety minutes later, a lone figure approached the perimeter of the force field and stopped.

Knoble rose and greeted the visitor. "Good evening, Colonel. My name is Alex Knoble and these people are the leaders of the protesters. We've come to discuss a way for you to save face, save your command, and a way out of this quagmire your mercenaries have created."

The Colonel was incensed. "Mr. Knoble you don't seem to realize the trouble you're in. I could have you..."

Knoble interrupted, "No, you can't and no, you won't. Colonel, you don't seem to understand the situation you and your men are in, in this theater of operation. So let me lay it out for you. This entire square city block has been sealed by a force field. No one gets in or out. Your command and communications have been disabled. Any aerial assets you might have had are grounded.

On our walk over here from S.W. Salmon Avenue, we encountered a number of your troopers. Over two-thirds of your battalion has now been quarantined and can no longer help you. You are unable to call for reinforcements. And all of this has been transmitted to the world via the World Wide Web in high resolution audio and video in real time. The news media is having a field day with this, and you and your command are coming under some very close scrutiny. And even after the revelation of our force field, people are going to wonder why you had to bring so much firepower against a group of unarmed, peaceful civilians who posed no threat to you or your men.

Now," he paused, "shall we talk?"

"What do you want?" asked the Colonel belligerently.

"Why, the same thing you want, Colonel," replied Knoble, "an end to the riots and a return to normalcy in Portland."

"And how do you propose we do that?" grumbled the Colonel.

"I would respectfully request," suggested Knoble, "that when your command and communications is restored you withdraw all your men to this block to protect the Federal Building. You are, after all, 'Federal Agents.' I'm sure that both the mayor and the governor would agree to that. And the local police department can handle the peaceful protestors and the out-of-town rioters."

"I can't do that," shouted the Colonel. "They'll bust me down to private!"

"Colonel," snapped Knoble, "at the very least you will be fired from whatever company you work for. At worst, you'll be indicted for conspiracy. So you can make a command decision or we can put a call into the Department of Homeland Security Acting Secretary Wolf and see what he has to say — the decision is yours."

A decision was shortly made. Three hours later the 'captain' at the penalty box told his charges, "Gentlemen, you have been redeemed and are being released into the custody of your Colonel. The chain attached to your ankles carries ten thousand volts of electricity...more than enough to incapacitate all of you instantly. If even one of you steps out of line by more than a foot, you all go down. You are your brother's keepers. It's bad enough that you're having to walk to the Federal Building in your skivvies, let's not compound that by your having to be dragged, unconscious, through the streets by a tractor."

By the time the docile soldiers arrived at the Federal Building, Alpha Team2 had already been there and left two hundred fifteen boxes, one for each soldier, containing their uniforms, weapons, and personal effects and a completed inventory list. Both the mayor of Portland and the Governor of Oregon went on national TV applauding the assistance of an unnamed citizen's group and the leaders of the protesters.

The local police department quickly reasserted itself. Alex Knoble, his teams and the force field, left Portland and quietly returned to their homes without ever being arrested or prosecuted.

Quiet and calmness slowly returned to Portland. The news media reported, two weeks later, that there hadn't been one riot in the time since the Federal Agents were withdrawn.

The President triumphantly tweeted about the tremendous victory of Federal Agents over the anarchists and leftist protesters in Portland.

About the Author

A little older and a lot grayer but still pushing on.

During the days of the past twenty-nine years, Dru has been a mild-mannered Macintosh computer maven. His company, Mac Help Desk [www.machelpdesk.com], continues to provide on-site Support, Sales, Training, and Service in the Macintosh and iDevice environments.

For more than fifteen years, Dru has been part of an international writing group called *Brainz*. Each month the group is charged with writing something — prose, poetry, short story, a song, screenplay — anything really, based on a one-word topic. Previous topics have included: mourning, fear, scars, numbers, and flying. Many of the stories in this book are generated from that group.

Dru lives in Richardson, Texas (a suburb of Dallas), with wifey Ava, and their four-legged love child, a standard poodle named Jacob.